In-Between

Speed beyond the speed of light.

by Tom Ryscavage

DORRANCE
PUBLISHING CO
EST. 1920
PITTSBURGH, PENNSYLVANIA 15238

Dorrance Publishing Co
585 Alpha Drive
Suite 103
Pittsburgh, PA 15238
Visit our website at *www.dorrancebookstore.com*

ISBN: 979-8-88925-344-0
eISBN: 979-8-88925-844-5

In-Between
Speed beyond the speed of light.

Table of Contents

PREFACE

Pure joy. Pure, pure joy. Am I floating? Maybe it does not mean anything whether I am or I am not floating. It is as if every part of me senses a gentle wave that brings the feeling of peace. I do not move. It moves. It moves through every part of me. The beautiful color of pearl white lingers everywhere. Where does it come from? I am not creating the beautiful white light. It is simply where I am.

The gentle movement that I sense is always there. I do not know. There is a light, pale blue light moving through the pearl white presence for only a brief moment, but then it is gone. What is it?

We are all together. I know this because nothing else can be true. Together. I just know we are together. Something that is far, far away from me is right beside me and it is with me.

Our shape is what everything wishes it to be. Gently changing. Always together. No sound but rather a feeling. I feel it is coaxed from me by everything around me. When I feel it, I know that it is happiness. Each one of us wants to spend every moment thanking the totality of what allows us to be who and where we are.

We ask for nothing. We give anything. We are. It has been this way forever. There is no past and there will be no future. Everything is now.

What did I just feel? Or did I hear something? Or both? A sound from somewhere. It made everything shudder.

Am I moving? No. Yes, everything is moving. Why? For what purpose is this?

Everything is moving downward. Far ahead I can feel something. It is nothing that I know. We are rushing toward it. Everything is just rushing toward it.

Something is pulling us toward some unknown place and it keeps increasing and increasing and increasing in strength. The dark point where we are being pulled has no white. It is the opposite. What is going on? Why is this happening?

The size of what is ahead keeps increasing. I see a black point that keeps enlarging. There was nothing there. Now this darkness is there. All I know is that everything is changing. Our motion has gone far beyond anything we could ever imagine. We are heading directly into the change. Why?

Chapter 1

I know she's there. She is standing in the doorway right behind me. I just know. She makes no sound. I just know she's there, Jimmy Loftus thinks with a mild smile on his face.

"I know you're there, Mom," Jimmy quietly says.

Silence. Jimmy doesn't turn around. His suitcase is on the bed. He just keeps folding his shirt and then fitting it into his suitcase. He tosses in some socks and then a sweater. He's packing to head back to college. It is early October and he had come home to spend the weekend with his family. It is early Sunday morning. His mother, Joanie, is a doctor and she left a few hours ago to go to the hospital to see her patients. She came into his room with a quiet knock earlier and kissed him on his forehead asking him to be safe with his drive back to Boston. His dad, Jack, is an engineer. He teaches at Williams College. He works at least part time for the US government and sometimes Jimmy thinks that he may actually work more than "part time" for the government. He seems to do many "research" trips for someone. He never speaks explicitly as to what they entail. He left an hour earlier to go to church.

"I know you're there, Mom," he quietly says again.

He is talking to his grandmother. Her name is Matilda but everyone in the family from her children to their children to their children call her "Mom." Friends and neighbors call her Tillie, but to be honest they wish they could call her "Mom." There is something different about Tillie. Jimmy has heard many explanations as to "why" she is different, but none really explain it.

She is in her eighties now, but not Jimmy nor anyone else can picture her looking any different in the past than how she looks right now. Long gray hair combed up into a bun. Intense blue-gray eyes. A beautiful face with the mouth that you could never quite tell what she is thinking. She went to high school, they think. If you are talking to her and never asked, you would assume that she has a PhD in something, but you are never quite sure what subject. Jimmy's best friend from school tells him that she thinks *"laterally."*

Jimmy slowly turns around and of course there she is quietly standing in the doorway to his bedroom looking right into his eyes. It is her eyes that fixate you. His friend from college, Mark, once said, *"Tillie's eyes take you on trips to very interesting places."*

"Why are you going back to school?" she asks.

Jimmy is in his junior year at MIT. He studies astrophysics.

"You know, Mom. I always must keep learning," Jimmy answers.

"Astrology," Mom says.

"Not astrology, Mom. Astrophysics. I study how the universe works. You know. I study stars and planets and waves and galaxies and black holes and things like that," Jimmy says.

"Like I said… astrology," Mom quietly replies.

Jimmy laughs.

"There are many days when that is exactly what I think, Mom."

His bag is packed and he picks it up and turns to the door to go downstairs and she is gone. He carries the bag down the steps, then down the side hallway to the kitchen. He still cannot find her. He goes out the kitchen door into the backyard and to his car. He pops the trunk and puts his suitcase in there. He turns around and there she is.

"Where did you learn to do that, Mom?" Jimmy asks.

"Do what?" Mom responds.

With a smile on his face, Jimmy just stares at her, thinking oh how much he loved this woman.

Jimmy leans over and gives Mom a kiss on her forehead. He gets into the car and puts the window down. He turns the car on and Mom comes over to the window.

"Mom, please tell Joan and Dad that I love them and I'll miss them all. I'll miss you the most, Mom. I'll be back for Thanksgiving. Also, *if* you talk to my sister, please tell her the same," Jimmy says. His sister is in her freshman year in college in Colorado.

Mom asks, "Will Mark and Paul come with you for Thanksgiving?"

Mark is Jimmy's best friend from college. He is one year ahead of Jimmy at MIT. He also is working for an initial BS in astrophysics. Paul is Mark's age and is one of his best friends. He studies economics at Harvard. They have in the past come to town several times with Jimmy for holidays over the past few years. Mark's family is from Florida. However, they have homes in three different States. Apparently, they are quite wealthy. Paul's family is from Montana. Both are planning to come to Jimmy's house for the Thanksgiving holiday. Jimmy is sure that their decision is not because of the food. He is quite certain that both Mark and Paul's families make quite a bit of money and they probably have chefs preparing their large family meals.

It is also not because they dislike their families. They do get home and they spend time with them. Oddly enough Jimmy keeps thinking it may be because of Mom. He remembers the last visit when they were here. The three of them, Mom, Mark, and Paul were in the small room located just off the living room. It is called the reading room. With their heads very close to one another they were talking about something for close to two hours. Jimmy never asked them what they were talking about and they never mentioned it

He says, "Mom, I'm pretty sure both of them are going to be coming for Thanksgiving." A soft smile comes across her face.

Jimmy leans out of the car window and says, "I'll write you a note each week to keep you, other Mom, Dad, and even Emily, if she comes home, up to date, Mom."

She looks intensely at Jimmy and then says something that puzzles him. She says, "Jimmy, I want you to always remember something. Remember what he told us. We must only go to the narrow gate."

Jimmy looks at her quizzically and says, "I'll remember that, Mom."

He starts the car and backs it down onto the alley behind their house and heads back to Boston.

Chapter 2

Jimmy turns off of Main Street and onto Patton Street and decides to head out of town by using the Burma trail. That is a winding road that weaves its way up into the mountains. It was named Burma trail by soldiers coming back from the Pacific arena of World War II. He could have gone on Main Street and straight up the mountain to where Main Street meets the interstate highway. He would have been back to Boston in two and a half hours. The road that he chose is a side road and will add an hour of beautiful scenery onto his trip. As he drives from Claire to Boston, enjoying every segment of the trip, it will take more than three hours.

Jimmy puts down the windows in his car and drives along at about 35 mph. He never sees another car. Probably because it is Sunday morning. The morning where everyone disappears. The road weaves its way up the mountain. He comes to an open field tucked into the mountains and then begins to reach forested areas. The trees are a mixture of conifers and deciduous. Long ago, most of the trees were white pine, but around the turn of the nineteenth century most were logged out. Except for some areas far up in the mountains where the logging industry never reached, there are groves of white pine that still flourish.

The trees are dense. The forest is made up of some white pine, blue spruce, and maple. There is some black walnut and chestnut and even some elm still scattered through the forest. As Jimmy cruises along the winding road, he takes deep breaths pulling in the beautifully crisp air. He sees the very beginning of changes in color of the deciduous trees. He thinks two weeks from today everything will be coming into its true beauty with the orange leaves mixed in with the red, yellow, and the still-green leaves and needles. All will be distinct and swirling around one another.

The winding road turns left, then right, then left, then right with each turn coming about one to three miles from the last one. Temperature is perfect at 74°F, so it is still Indian summer. Still no cars or trucks or bicyclists appear. It is only Jimmy and this little piece of earth.

As he is coming out of one of the forested areas and into another open meadow, he thinks he sees a flash in the distant sky just beyond the next forest. He thinks, *must be an airplane,* as he rolls past that meadow and continues into the next forest and then heads back out into another meadow. The open area meadows are bright and the forests are dark. After a mile or so, he keeps glancing to the left into each meadow. He thinks he would be able to see the plane that he saw flash, but there is nothing in the sky other than the intense Arizona deep blueness. Just before he enters the next forested area, he thinks he sees that flash again. It is not white but actually a silver tint. Oddly, he thought he saw it, but then it seemed to disappear. He is trying to keep his eyes on the road, but he keeps glancing off to the left even more so than before and the flash seems to be where it was the first time he thought that he saw it. Actually, it is staying in place. He thinks probably it was a silver balloon or a helicopter or drone or something. It didn't seem to move.

His car begins to leave the next wooded area and he turns and looks directly into the meadow. In an instant his foot is pressing on the brakes of the car and the car swerves off to the right of the road in a whirlwind of dust and gravel coming to a complete stop. He is looking straight ahead into the dust and his heart is beating at an intense rate. He slowly turns his head and looks into the meadow on his left. His mind isn't thinking at all. He is fixated on what is steady in the sky above the meadow. About 100 yards above the ground, there is a silvery triangular object. It is huge. Each of its three sides are about 200 yards long. Each side is about 100 yards high. The triangular-shape does not come to points at its ends. More so the ends are rounded. It is simply sitting in the sky. There are no visible windows or doors. Suddenly it disappears and just as quickly it reappears about 200 yards farther back in the meadow.

Jimmy slowly gets out of the car, keeping his eyes on this object. He then begins to cross the road and walk into the meadow. The object disappears once again and then reappears almost directly over top of him about fifty yards off the ground. He feels no change in temperature. Jimmy feels no heat nor cold coming off the object. There is absolutely no sound. Even the meadow produces no sound. As he looks even closer at the surface of the object, he suddenly realizes that the metal may be in a liquid form. Once again, the object disappears and then reappears just as quickly about 300 yards farther back in the meadow at a height of about 200 yards. Then slowly the object begins to turn in a circle on itself. Jimmy realizes that except for the top of the object he still has seen no breaks in the metal surface. The object then begins to slowly rise higher and then faster and then in the blink of an eye with no sound, no heat, no disturbance of the air it goes straight up into the sky, getting smaller as it rise until it disappears. Jimmy then collapses into a sitting position in the meadow and asks out loud, "What did I just see?"

CHAPTER 3

On Collier Street in Cambridge, Massachusetts stakes are high. In the apartment at the dining room table a seven card-high-low stud poker game is in progress. The players are all students at MIT. They make up a mixture of years from undergraduate to graduate studies. Two seniors, Mark O'Donnell and Sean, and two juniors, Terry and Jack, are staring at the table. The exposed cards stare back.

Jack says, "Well, Mark, it looks like you have that famous hand aces and eights."

Mark keeps staring at his cards and whispers, "Aces over eights." He then moves five bottle caps into the center of the table and states, "I'll raise you five beers." The other three players respond the same.

Mark then says, "Speaking of beers, I'm going to go grab one. Do any of you kindergarteners need one to increase your luck?"

There were no requests from the competitors.

Mark gets up and goes into the laundry room, which is just off the kitchen. He lifts up the door on the top of the clothes washing machine. The machine is full to the top with ice and beer. He grabs an ice cold Yuengling beer bottle and heads back toward the dining room.

At that moment the front door to the apartment opens and Jimmy walks in. When Mark sees him, he pauses and calls, "Hey, Jim, every-thing okay?"

Jimmy's face is pale and he is staring directly ahead toward the stairs. He doesn't respond and starts up the steps. Jimmy turns to face him and says, "Come upstairs with me."

The two of them go up the steps and go to Jimmy's room and he sits down on the edge of his bed. Mark leans against the dresser, crosses his arms and asks, "Jimmy, is everybody okay at home?" He continues, "Mom is okay, right? Your parents, sis, all okay, right?"

Jimmy doesn't say anything. He just keeps staring straight ahead.

Mark says, "Jimmy, what's going on?"

Jimmy suddenly looks at Mark and says, "Sorry, no, everybody is fine."

He pauses again and then he begins to explain the entire day to Mark. He describes everything that he saw right up to where the object flew directly up into the sky at an enormous speed.

Mark says, "What do you think you were seeing? Some sort of an aircraft? You know, Jimmy, sometimes we see things in the sky that are things we have never seen before, but they are normal things and our mind plays tricks on us. It makes us create situations that are not even there."

Jimmy doesn't say anything for a bit and then says, "Mark, what I told you I saw, I actually saw. It was real. I was right underneath it and at one point it could not have been more than thirty yards away from me."

This time Mark doesn't say anything. He is simply staring at Jimmy and then he straightens up from leaning on the dresser and says, "Okay, let's figure this out. Now, Jimmy, I'm going to ask you questions and I want you to close your eyes and go back into that field. First tell me again about what you thought was the structure of this vessel. You said it almost looked like liquid metal. Explain that to me."

Jimmy says, "It was definitely metal. You can tell that from the semi-shine, but as I got closer it actually seemed to be moving metal. Do you know what I mean?"

Mark asks, "Like mercury?"

Jimmy says, "Yes but a much slower movement and it had a duller shine than Mercury. I guess what I'm saying is that it gave the impression that even though I was looking at a triangular structure, it was flexible. Maybe it could change shape."

Mark asks, "Did you see that happen?"

Jimmy responds, "No, I think it was the smoothness of everything. There were no sharp points nor sharp angles. No edges. Everything was rounded at endpoints. If you have something like that made out of liquid metal there would be nothing stopping it from changing shape. If you made a triangular-shaped bagel out of liquid metal that's what it would look like, but it was so smooth."

Mark then says, "I'm going to ask you a question and I want you to think very hard about your answer. You said it kept disappearing and then reappearing. Is that correct?"

Jimmy answers, "Yes, it would disappear and almost instantaneously reappear, but it would reappear somewhere else."

Mark asks, "You are sure that it was just disappearing and not moving at an unbelievable high speed, right?"

Jimmy says, "I thought about that on my way here. I wondered if my human eyes were incapable of determining the difference between the two. Was it disappearance or extraordinary speed? I believe it was disappearing and reappearing."

Mark continues asking him about the actual structure of the object. He keeps coming back to the absence of anything to indicate entrances or exits or wheels or windows or functional structures of any type. Mark asks, "Now, I know this is very hard to answer, but do you think someone was piloting this vessel?"

Jimmy answers, "That was my impression. There was something inside of it. Flying it. The thing was so large."

After more questioning, Mark tells Jimmy, "To be very honest with you, Jim, if I were hearing this from someone other than you, I would worry. However, I know you well enough and I believe you saw what you saw and it was real. You already know that in our field there are little quips made about situations like this and that people like you and I would be the ones to make them. There are three things that you have mentioned that I've heard many times when I read about people who claim to have seen these objects. Those things are the triangular-shape, the incredible speed, but most of all the disappearance and reappearance. Others have seen that and it would make listeners think the person was crazy or not telling the truth. To me, however, that is the one thing that I have heard or read over and over again concerning UFO sightings that actually made me think that this is possibly real because it is the appearance and disappearance that I believe is the key to the mystery. A new aspect of chemistry, physics, astrophysics which has never been considered will need to now be considered."

Jimmy sighs. "Is this going to adversely affect how I think about anything that we are taught from this point on?"

Mark answers, "No not at all. You, me, Paul, and other guys have talked about it many times. Our professors tend to think in limitations, but as students, we are still searching. We do not believe in limitations. There is always an answer. I have always thought that whatever gift that Tillie possesses you must have inherited it. I will tell you one thing and that is you have just directed me into a world of work and I promise you I will solve it, and when I do, you will be the first to know. Both of us must remain quiet about this for now. I believe everything that you have told me. However, I now have to prove it to myself."

Chapter 4

Ten years later, two men are sitting across from each other in an open booth at a popular restaurant in New York City. The younger of the two, Nate, asks, "Well, Bill, so is this your last case?"

Bill responds, "That's my plan." He then quickly asks Nate, "What is the guy doing? Is he just sitting there?"

They are talking about a person who is sitting alone at a table located fairly close to Bill and Nate. The person is Dr. James Loftus. For the past six years, Jimmy has been doing work in astrophysics for the United States Government. If you work for the government and you have a high enough clearance level for sensitive information, you are periodically reassessed. You require "clearance" for approval for the intelligence level that you hold. Jimmy went through this when he started his current occupation with the government. That was five years ago. He is due for his next reassessment. He was told at the beginning of his employment that he would be reassessed every five years and sometimes even more frequently depending upon exactly where the intelligence level in his present work may be. It is simply working for the government.

Jimmy has been working on the Mars Project. Specifically, he has been working on transport from Earth to Mars. The United States and other governments from around the world have reached the point where each aspect of the journey to and back from Mars is nearly complete.

Jimmy's cell phone rings. He takes it from his coat pocket and hits the Receive button and says, "Hey, Mimi. Everything okay?" Mimi's real name is Melinda. She is Jimmy's wife.

He listens for a moment, then says, "No, I'm not at the conference now. I finished up about forty minutes ago. I'm grabbing a quick bite to eat at Du Midi restaurant." They've been married a little over seven years and have one child. The child's name is Lily.

Jimmy continues and says, "I've finished up my work here and I'll be heading back down to Washington tomorrow morning. I'll be on the morning seven o'clock train so I'll be getting there around noon. I'll take a cab home from Union Station."

Mimi says something and Jimmy responds, "Don't worry. I'll find something to do and I'll see you when you get back from your chores." Mimi also works for the government. She is an analyst at the NSA. She will be starting a two-week vacation on Monday.

Jimmy says, "You want me to pick Lily up at school?" Mimi responds and Jimmy says, "Great. Tell her to look for me outside the school." He says, "Love you." And hangs up.

Bill asks Nate in a whisper, "Anything interesting?"

Nate says, "He was talking to his wife. I guess his work up at NYU is wrapped up for now and he's heading back to DC tomorrow."

Bill then says, "Just imagine. A few months from now I may be sitting in a canoe at my cottage on Lake Penn."

Nate asks, "Fishing?"

"Nope. Just sitting in the canoe floating around appreciating the breeze—"

Suddenly there is a loud crash. Something had fallen behind Nate. Sounded like broken glass and dishes. Bill looks to see and Nate turns around to see as well. There is a busboy kneeling down, putting pieces of broken dishes and glass onto his large round tray.

When Nate turns back to look at Bill, he then notices someone standing in front of Jimmy's table. Nate then notices the look on Jimmy's face. It's as if Jimmy is seeing a ghost. Nate begins fumbling with his pen that is actually an extremely sensitive microphone. He begins turning the pen to home in on the conversation between this person and Jimmy.

The person standing in front of Jimmy says, "Well, Jim, it's great seeing you again."

Jimmy then says, "Mark, where in the name of God have you been? I've been looking for you for ten years. I've tried calling. I've sent letters. They weren't returned, but there was no response. I sent them to your parents' home up in Albany and in Florida. I tried to find Paul. Couldn't find him. I'd ask our friends from school if they knew anything. Some people would have little snippets of information that you were working on some project for the government but then others would say no not the government. It's more likely just some private consulting. Nobody knew for sure. I'd give up for a while, but then I'd start looking again."

Jimmy continues, "I heard that your parents passed away about nine years ago. Someone had just mentioned that to me about a year after it happened. I thought for a while that you were angry that I didn't attend the funeral but, Mark, I never knew. Also, you missed my wedding," Jimmy whispers.

Mark says, "I know this sounds crazy, but I was at your wedding. I didn't go to the reception, though. I was at the church."

"Paul was there too. Our wives as well."

Jimmy says, "You're married? I'm becoming extremely angry. You sound like a person who's in hiding. What is going on? What are you doing?"

"Jimmy," Mark says in a low voice, "do you remember the last thing I said to you at my graduation?"

Jimmy does remember.

"You said the same thing to me that day that you told me nine months before in my bedroom at the house in Cambridge." Jimmy slowly says, "You promised me that when you've solved this problem, you would explain everything to me. Right?"

Mark says, "That's right and what I said is true. That is why I'm here." Mark reaches inside his jacket and pulls out a small, clear glass tube. The tube is filled with liquid. There are two levels of fluid. Colorless liquid is on the bottom half and blue tinged liquid on the top half. He holds the tube up in front of Jimmy.

At the FBI agents' table, Nate is trying to see what Mark is holding up in front of Jimmy, but he cannot quite see it.

Mark says, "This is it."

Jimmy says, "What are you—"

Mark breaks in and whispers, "Jimmy, the clear fluid is oil and the blue fluid is water but you already know that... right?"

Jimmy says, "Obviously."

Mark says, "Lean toward me."

Jimmy leans forward and Mark whispers in his ear. He continues whispering and there is no expression on Jimmy's face. Mark then shakes up the tube and Jimmy's eyes widen.

They pull away from each other and continue talking in a normal voice.

At the table near them, the man with his back toward Jimmy and Mark whispers, "What did he say?"

The other man says, "I couldn't hear it. I sure wish I had a more powerful sound amplifier."

The older man says, "But you had the pen turned on maximum, right?"

The other man says, "Yes. Maybe the techs can make it out better."

At the other table Mark has a sly smile on his face and Jimmy's eyes are still wide open.

Jimmy asks, "How fast?"

Mark answers, "If you have an engine, let's say from a lawn mower, you could achieve speeds far, far, far beyond the speed of light. So, imagine the speed from that point with more powerful thrust."

Jimmy asks, "How do you determine—?"

Mark interrupts. "Everything will be shown to you on the chips that you'll have received."

Jimmy asks, "What chips?" Then Jimmy says, "About what I saw… did you meet them? Talk to them?"

Mark says, "That's not important because—"

Jimmy interrupts and says, "What do you mean it's not important? Of course, it has to be important. Isn't that what this is all about?"

Mark says, "Jimmy, trust me. The question that you're asking is truly not important in the sense of how you're asking it. Imagine if your wife and daughter and you decided to drive from here in New York City to Los Angeles—"

Jimmy interrupts by saying, "You know that I have a daughter?"

Mark continues, "You all get in your car and leave from Third Avenue to the Lincoln Tunnel into New Jersey and then get on Interstate 80 and you take that across New Jersey into Pennsylvania. You get as far as a town, let's say Williamsport, Pennsylvania, and you notice your fuel is getting a little low so you get off the highway and go to a gas station. You fill the tank. Your wife and daughter, Mimi and Lily go into the gas station to get some snacks and then come back to the car. They get in and you top off the tank. You use a credit card to pay for the gas. Then you get in your car. You leave the station and you're on your way heading west. What do you expect to happen at that gas station after you leave? Are the neighbors going to come in to ask the owners of the gas station who you were? Where were you going? Do you live around here?" Mark continues with "Is that what you expect to happen if you went on that trip?"

Jimmy says no.

Mark says, "That's what you asked me and that is what I meant." He continued. "Exactly what is happening is rather complex… to some people. However, everything that I just told you about your trip is extremely important. Which route, the gas tank, the available gas, the snacks, your planned route but most important is the destination. Always remember, Jimmy, everything that I've talked about has a reason. All of the information that you'll have received is dependent on what I just showed you in the bottle.

"I call it the 'In Between' and that is not a theory. It is real. 'In Between' is a place. Everyone is fixated on how you travel. It has very little to do with how. It has to do with where. The where is 'In Between.' I just showed you exactly what the 'In Between' actually is. The two liquids. Each one knows that the other is there but they have virtually nothing to do with each other except that they exist. They are there and they cannot interact with each other except that each *is* there. It is the presence of one that affects the other."

Mark leaned forward and whispered in Jimmy's ear, "What is frequently ignored is that there is always a space between them. It is that space that answers so many of the questions."

Bill and Nathan are listening as intently as they can, but they cannot hear clearly enough to really understand everything that Jimmy and Mark are discussing.

Suddenly there is a smash of glass again behind them and they turn to look. It is a busboy who had dropped another glass on the floor. The busboy is looking at them with a slight smile on his face.

They both quickly turn and look at Jimmy's table. Jimmy is alone at the table. They then look toward the entrance to the restaurant and see Mark walking out the front door. They also look on their table and see a piece of paper. Nathan picks it up. Written on the small piece is a note that said: *Too late*.

They look at each other and Bill gets up and heads toward the door.

Once Mark is outside of the restaurant, he quickly gets into a cab. He hops into the back of the cab and says to the driver to "Make a right here at the corner." As his cab gets to the corner, he sees Bill come out of the restaurant. Bill looks and sees him in the cab as it makes a right-hand turn.

Bill hails a cab and jumps in and says, "Follow the cab in front of us."

As Mark's cab approaches the corner, he gives the cabbie $50 and tells him, "Shortly after this turn, slow down. I'm getting out, but I want you to continue straight up Third Avenue until you use up your $50, okay?"

The cabbie answers, "Okay." Once their cab completes the right-hand turn, the cabbie slows down to almost a stop and Mark opens the door and gets out of the cab and steps into the shadows against the buildings.

His cabbie continues up Third Street.

Bill's cab then makes the right-hand turn. Bill sees Mark's cab heading up Third Avenue and his cab follows.

Once Bill's cab has gone far enough up the street Mark walks out of the shadows. He crosses the street and slowly meanders west along Fourteenth Street.

CHAPTER 5

The following morning in a controlled office room in the Ronald Regan building in Washington, DC, a meeting was held. Bill and Nate sat around a table with a man, Agent George Haas from the CIA. At the table there were two other persons—a man from the FBI, Mr. Smith and one woman from the Department of Defense, Major Micki Pflueger. The FBI agents had met each of these individuals before.

Agent Haas speaks to Bill and Nate, "Just tell Major Pflueger and Mr. Smith what happened during your evening in New York."

Bill and Nate then ran through the entire scene at the restaurant. They explained everything except for their chatter before the appearance of Mark. They covered everything as best as they could remember it. They then played the enhanced version of their audio tape.

Mr. Smith from the CIA remained quiet. Major Pflueger asked them, "You never knew who Mark was, is that correct?"

Bill answers and says, "Initially, I could not recognize him because my back was facing toward their table. Nate could see him, but Nate has not been on this case very long. It took me a little bit of time, but then I remembered reading about Mark being his best friend back when Jimmy was at MIT. I made the assumption that is who it was. I know that when Dr. Loftus first got his contract to work for the government

Mark was interviewed in that intake information. Now, once again, I am assuming that it was Mark. Mark as I suspect you all know comes from a very wealthy family. They were respected in our government. Both parties have been thankful to them for donations and occasional work for the government.

"His parents died in an automobile accident about one year after Mark's graduation from MIT. He was an only child and upon their death he received their estate. It was an enormous fortune. He went to Stanford to receive his masters in astrophysics and then the doctorate as well. Apparently, he is a very intelligent person. He received those degrees rather quickly. After receiving his doctorate, it was almost as if he disappeared. He could be, however, located if anybody had any reason to look. He wasn't hiding. He was simply more distant. Some people thought that he was just enjoying his wealth, but actually he was involved in private research. Very secretive research, actually, because for a long time no one really knew what research he was doing. We also were able to determine that he was performing incredible studies into odd metals."

Agent Haas then turned to Major Pflueger and Mr. Smith. He began by asking both of them, "You have had some contact with Mark during the past few years. Is that correct?"

Mr. Smith answered first, stating, "We had heard that he was doing research on the ability to detect any object moving within a mile of a central point. We were interested as was Major Pflueger's department with this type of detection range. Our department was aware of the location where he was doing his research. Oddly, his research lab was rather deep in the woods. To be exact the lab was located up against the side of a mountain. His research center was actually carved into the mountain."

Agent Haas then asked him how this group were able to deliver all of their research equipment to a site so remote?

Smith raised his hand and rubbed his thumb and index finger together. He then said, "He apparently is quite wealthy. To be honest with you we were more interested in how far he had developed this detection system. He said it was almost complete but the one agent said he had a strong feeling that it was quite complete."

The woman asked, "Why did he think that?"

Mr. Smith said, "While the agents were in one of his labs, he showed them a tape of the two agents from that day. It showed, in detail, the two agents beginning over a mile away from his laboratory. It was not a video. It was a three dimensional picture of the two agents coming up the mountain in their car and walking the path back toward the lab. It was a three dimensional!"

The woman asked, "They were sure it was not a video?"

Mr. Smith said, "Phillips and one of his group told the agent the image can be in any form that they wished, but what they were looking at was not video."

The woman asked, "What?"

Mr. Smith said, "They saw extremely intricate computers in the lab when they were shown the tracking. On one of his computers he was able to show the agents they were tracking as dots and sounds or fully three-dimensional figures that looked awfully close to what the two agents actually looked like as they made their way through the forest heading toward his lab.

The major asked, "Did he explain how this was done?"

"Not really. He simply said that they had constructed a way to detect the slightest motion," the agent answered.

Phillips then said, "Everything is alive in different ways, even stones, and if something passes by and moves a blade of grass or a leaf or piece of sand, energy is interfered with and this change is passed on to the surrounding, living things. If you could detect all of the interference you can, with the correct software see what did it and where it was done. I know that people have tried to do this for quite some time and they thought that with more powerful sensors they would be able to do it, but he explained in actuality what you want is extremely weak sensors and a method to pass the information from where it is happening to your central point of search. This was the method that he had determined."

Obviously, the agents were rather impressed. They asked him if he would share this information with the government. He said no problem and to my knowledge he has already forwarded almost all of his research.

Smith asked, "Who received this project?"

The CIA man said, "Apparently, it's at the farm." He continued, explaining that "they are astounded as to the sensitivity and accuracy of this detecting process. They already have it up in numerous areas around the farm."

"Was it extremely expensive?" asked Smith.

The man from the CIA said, "Our economic advisors are working out a cost with him. He's not trying to make money from this new system. He just seemed interested in helping our government."

Smith said, "I assume therefore he's gone through the evaluation process, is that correct?"

Major Pflueger said, "We handled that and it's been a few years since the evaluation was done. Nobody found anything, but that's where we found out that he was also doing a tremendous amount of research into metals."

Smith asked, "Did you ask him why he was doing that type of research?"

Pflueger said yes. She then continued, saying, "He just said that new metals are always something that we should be looking for to make everything that we construct in science. We wish them to perform at their best. "Our agents just thought he was talking about this detection system."

Smith then said, "And this is why we're here today because apparently his detection system was not the only thing he was creating." He continued adding, "So we ask each other what was he doing?"

The CIA agent said, "We sent the same two agents back to his laboratory this morning and they shall be in touch with us after they assess the situation."

Smith then said, "Okay, that's it for today, but I'd like to meet tomorrow in this office at 8:00 A.M." He continued while looking at the FBI agents, "You have Dr. Loftus in the crosshairs, don't you?"

The older FBI agent answered, "Dr. Loftus and his wife and child are under complete watch. Phones, mail, computers, both at home and at work. Agents rented a room near his house here in DC. They can see everyone who comes and goes. He is in the cone. If Mark said that he would be receiving all of his research, then we will intercept it."

Agent Smith then says, "Right now we're not ready to talk to Dr. Loftus about this situation. There are too many questions to be answered first."

CHAPTER 6

Jimmy did not sleep well that night. He just kept going over everything that happened the night before. He totally trusts Mark but since both are scientists, their thinking is more vertical thinking. He cannot look at the situation where A is followed by D. It has to be predictable. Therefore, it has to go A-B-C-D. He is not seeing that yet.

Mark said that he would get all of his research to Jimmy, but he said nothing as to when, where, how. He left no contact numbers. He left no addresses. He left no internet sites.

Then there was the confusion in the restaurant. The smashed glass just before he showed up at his table. The smashed glass just as he disappeared.

Sitting in the table just in front of his were two men. As Mark quickly left the restaurant Jimmy could swear he saw him drop a piece of paper onto their table. One of them got up to follow Mark. Who were they? Too many questions.

Jimmy goes through automatic checkout from the hotel. He then asks the front desk to have a taxi ready for him in fifteen minutes. He had packed the night before and he heads down to the lobby. The cab arrives and he tells the driver to take him to Penn Station.

It is a very early Sunday morning but activity in New York City is already beginning to pick up. The horns, the motors, the yelling all make quite a unique mixture of sounds, but there is no cohesion of the sounds.

Penn Station was mildly crowded. His train would be leaving for Washington, DC at 7:00 A.M.

He got on one of the reserved cars of the train. He settled into his seat. The train leaves on time. Once the train is out of the city the food car opens. He got up and got himself a cup of coffee. As he headed back to his seat, he noticed a middle-aged man in a seat across the aisle from him. He stared at him, but the man never made any eye contact.

The trip from New York City to Washington, DC in a train is rather relaxing. Driving in a car is anything but relaxing. So, Jimmy just sat back looking out the window, but this trip was different from previous trips. From a train window you can see how certain areas of the country are doing economically. You get to see companies that are up and blooming or closed and dismantling. You pass historic areas during the trip and your mind will quickly go back to those times and you keep bringing up even more questions that were not answered in your history classes.

Not this day. His mind was still on last night.

He arrived at Union Station in DC and took a cab up to Chevy Chase, Maryland. This is where he resides. He walked into the front door. He heard his wife Melinda in the kitchen. She heard him come in and called out his name. He dropped his bag and walked into the kitchen and held her tightly and gave her a kiss and said, "I missed you. I thought that you would be out getting chores accomplished."

Melinda pulled back a little bit, tilted her head with a quizzical look on her face, and said, "You normally forget to say that when you come back from your trips. Is everything okay?"

Jimmy said, "I think it's okay and I have a very interesting story to tell you and maybe we can go out for lunch. Where is Lily?"

Melinda said, "I think she's downstairs in the playroom with her friend Nora." Jimmy smiles. He likes Nora. She is always chewing gum, but she is an incredibly intelligent girl.

He says to Melinda, "I'm going to run down to Georgetown and go to mass at eleven. Maybe we can take the girls out to a restaurant of their choice after I get back?"

Melinda says, "That sounds great. I can put my dishwasher load away. I'll call Nora's parents and see if it's okay. You know I can make you a snack here instead of going to a restaurant?"

Jimmy says, "Something tells me that I should go to a restaurant. Don't ask me why because I have no idea why."

Melinda says, "Okay with me."

Jimmy didn't even put his luggage away. He just left it in the foyer. He grabbed his keys and went out to his garage located off the backyard. He hopped into his car and headed toward Georgetown.

Jimmy and his entire family as well as Melinda's family are all Catholics. He usually goes to church at Dahlgren Chapel on the campus of Georgetown University. He is, however, a parishioner at St. Vincent's Catholic Church, but the decreased size of Dahlgren has always been comforting to him. On many occasions he has wondered why he feels exactly where he needs to be, but he has never been able to understand why.

The real reason that he is going to Georgetown campus today is because there is a Jesuit priest, Cian Thorne with whom he needs to speak.

As it turns out, Father Thorne is the one who is actually celebrating the Mass. Once he was thinking about the number of Masses that he has attended during his life and wondering why the same ceremony presents itself as the First Mass. They say it is the mystery of faith. His mind settled on the Mass. After Mass he waited in the back of the chapel until Father Thorne came out of the Sacristy.

Father Thorne saw him. Jimmy waved and headed down the side aisle directly toward his friend. Father Thorne said, "Hey, Jimmy, what's up? Did I save your soul?"

Jimmy smiled. Father Cian Thorne is a person who has a perpetual smile on his face but not with his mouth or his cheeks. It is with his eyes. They are deep blue and full of life. Jimmy learned about looking into people's eyes when he did volunteer work during one summer. He worked at a prison near his home in western Massachusetts. If you look deep enough into someone's eyes you can learn an awful lot. In a prison you get a feeling rather quickly whether the person whom you are talking to doesn't belong there or whether he or she should be there for a long, long time. There is life and fulfillment or no life with just emptiness.

Looking into Father Thorne's eyes entraps you, no matter where you are at that moment, to somehow go where he is.

"Hey, Jimmy," and Father Thorne says, "Hey, Jimmy. Did our mothers know each other?"

Jimmy responds, "Never asked her."

"Nor did I," Father Thorne says with a smile. He continues, "What's on your mind?"

Jimmy responds, "Well, that's the confusing part. I'm not quite sure." He begins to describe to Father Thorne what happened over the weekend. He explained that he was at a conference in Manhattan and that he went to dinner at a restaurant after the meeting was concluded. He slowly told him about Mark showing up suddenly and how he had not seen him in ten years. He explained that he had many hidden resentments about Mark for exiting his life for such a long time, and then out of nowhere he shows up again.

Father Thorne said, "But from what you told me, if I get this right, he was watching you very closely but doing it invisibly. Is that right?"

Jimmy said, "Yes, that's how he explained it."

Father Thorne mused, "Jimmy, you know that there had to be a reason for him doing things that way, right?"

Jimmy quickly responds, "But I didn't know of any reason."

Father Thorne said, "That's what I'm saying. He cared enough about you to keep very close tabs on you, but maybe he was protecting you. Is that possible?"

Jimmy hesitates and then says, "I guess I'm going to have to tell you the whole story."

Jimmy then goes all the way back to when he met Mark and his friend Paul at MIT.

Father Thorne oddly held up his hand and said, "I have not heard of Mark, but I was a friend of Paul's if he's who I think you're referring to."

Father Thorne then describes his friend Paul McCabe and Jimmy said, "That has to be the same Paul."

Father Thorne says, "Paul and I were close friends all the way back to grade school. Small world, isn't it? I once knew a psychologist who used to swear that there were only 832 people in the entire world. That, however, is the easy explanation. There is a very specific reason for everything."

They both laughed.

Jimmy then continued explaining every part of his experience on that day when he drove from his home to his house in Cambridge, Massachusetts. He continued by explaining his entire conversation with Mark after he got back to his apartment. They were sitting in the pew in the back of the church. He told Father Thorne everything that he could remember about that day. He told him what he ended up seeing. He explained how he told Mark about this as soon as he got back to his apartment. He told him Mark's response. He then told him about last night in the restaurant. He told him about the little bottle with the water and oil that Mark showed him to explain… well, everything.

Jimmy paused and said, "Cian, I have to ask you to promise me that you will not tell anybody about what I'm about to tell you. Okay?"

Father Thorne answered, "Lips zipped."

Jimmy then explained to him what it was that Mark was really working on for those ten years and that he was certain that he had solved the problem of movement through space.

Father Thorne then asked, "And the solution was?"

Jimmy said, "That's one of the problems. I don't know. He said that I would receive all of his research. He didn't say when or how or what. He just said I would have it."

Father Thorne said, "Paul once described a friend of his named Mark. He said that the friend was a person who was a scientist, but he went beyond vertical thinking where A goes to B goes to C. He said his friend also thinks laterally were A goes to 28, which goes to the color yellow."

Jimmy says, "Like DeBono's Lateral Thinking."

"Correct," says Father Thorne. He continues, "Lateral thinking is closer to religious thinking than to scientific thinking. For example, 'An eye for an eye' is vertical thinking. But in our religion if you get slapped on your right cheek you turn your head so that they can slap you again on your left cheek. That's lateral thinking."

Jimmy quietly says, "It's all a mixture and you can see why I still don't know if it's an A or 29 or B or yellow or slap in the face."

Father Thorne then says, "I see the complexity. There is someone I want you to talk to. He is a Jesuit priest, but he is not here in Georgetown. His time is split between the Vatican and Tucson, Arizona."

"The Kitt Peak Observatories, correct?" Jimmy says.

Father Thorne says, "Yes. Will you promise to keep me up-to-date with what you find out? The reason why I ask you that will be explained to you in Tucson. I promise you that no one will hear what we've been talking about unless you tell me to share it. I have a rather powerful feeling that what just happened to you has happened to everyone a long, long time ago."

"I'll keep you up front, Jimmy. Except for Melinda, you're the first and only person so far that I've spoken to about this situation. There is a reason for that and I know you understand why I'm here today... besides Mass." He then smiles.

Chapter 7

Jimmy leaves Georgetown and heads back home to Chevy Chase. It is a relatively short drive and if you are aware of the side streets the travel time is about fifteen minutes. He pulls into the parking area in the back of their house. He goes through the garage, then the garden and lawn and through the back door into the kitchen. He hears a rhythmic beat coming from the living room. He goes that direction and finds his wife, Melinda, his daughter Emily, and his daughter's friend Nora. They are line dance to an exercise video on TV.

He smiles. Melinda catches his reflection, oddly enough, in the screen of the TV. One must be trained to be able to do something like that, especially when you are mentally involved in something else.

She turns around to him and smiles as do the little girls. Mimi reaches for the remote control and turns off the TV.

Jimmy says, "You never miss anything, do you?"

Just as her occupational training taught her, she just smiled.

Melinda is on leave from her current job out in Fort Meade, Maryland where she is employed by the NSA.

You may hear people in the intelligence field say that they are retired. No one ever retires from the intelligence field. They just say that. Melinda is not retired. She is on leave. She just wanted to spend more time with her daughter. At her office at the NSA, she investigates everything and everybody via cameras from outer space. The number of the satellites enwrapping our planet for photographic investigation is by far beyond the extent that anyone would estimate. As with all intelligence departments, everything is segmented. No one is sure what other people are doing or even what they can do. It is a secret. And everyone must keep the secret.

She is going on a two-week "vacation."

Jimmy asks, "Well, where have you and the girls decided that we will head for a bite to eat?"

Melinda responds, "I didn't decide at all.

The young girls loudly answered, "WE did!"

Melinda whispers, "They want to go to Tony's Pizza."

Jimmy says, "Fine with me."

They all get into the car. Melinda drives. Jimmy is in the passenger seat and the girls in the backseat of Melinda's Ford Eddie Bauer.

As they get on Connecticut Avenue and head toward Washington, DC, Jimmy was quietly explaining his conversation with Father Jimmy at Dahlgren Chapel. He says nothing about their discussion about Mark. She knows Father Jimmy quite well. As with all Jesuits they will turn up to be friends of your best friends. Probably more than anything, it is the Jesuits who keep bringing back to Jimmy's mind to what his psychologist friend once said about the 832 people in the world. When you speak to a Jesuit long enough you begin to realize that 832 number might be true.

They reached the restaurant and easily find seats. Jimmy begins in a low voice to discuss his conversation with Father Thorne.

However, after about fifteen minutes into the conversation Nora spoke up and said, "I know a Mark."

Jimmy says, "I'm sure you do, Nora. There are a lot of Marks in this world." He thinks that he must not have spoken as quietly as he thought he had.

Nora continues, "I heard you mention MIT. That's where my Mark went to school."

Jimmy asks, "What's his last name?"

Nora responds, "I've only known him as Mark. He's a friend of my dad's. They met when we were at the beach a few years ago."

Nora's father, David Cox, PhD, is a metallurgist.

Nora continues, "He's building something."

Melinda asks, "What is he building?"

Nora answers, "I'm not sure, but whatever it is it is quite important because when he and Dad talked about it, they were whispering just like Melinda and you were whispering."

Jimmy thinks that he has always thought that Nora was an exceptionally intelligent child, but it seems she has talents far beyond those found even in adults.

Jimmy asks, "What does he look like?"

Melinda and Jimmy begin to listen to a description of a person who is a twin to Jimmy's friend Mark, and Jimmy asks, "How long have you known him?"

Nora responds, "I guess four or five years."

Melinda asks, "That was the first time your parents met him?"

Nora answers, "Yep. Met him at the beach. But he has been to our house a few times."

Jimmy asks slowly, "When was the last time you saw him?"

Nora says, "Last week. He was only at our house for about an hour or two."

Melinda asks, "Why was he there?"

Nora answers, "I guess he came to talk to Dad."

Melinda asks, "Did he talk to you?"

Nora says, "Yep. For a little bit."

Jimmy says, "What did you talk to him about?"

Nora answers, "Well…," she pauses as if she's thinking and then says, "nothing important." She continues, "Like I said, he wasn't there very long, but when he left my dad and my mom over-hugged him. I heard them say to him that they will pray every day for him and they pleaded that they will see him again. Then he turned toward me and smiled and gave me the thumbs-up sign. Then he left."

Jimmy and Melinda were quiet.

They were served the pizza. The little girls were arguing over their favorite type of pizza. It is always so funny how every person would like a different topping on their pizza if they could get it. People taste things, smell things, hear things, and see things somewhat differently from each other. That may seem chaotic, but it is a blessing to humans to never allow someone else to tell you what you like. By far Americans have that flaw down to perfection.

When they were finished eating, they drove back to their home and parked the car but before Jimmy or Melinda got out of the car, Melinda said, "Let's not talk about this for a little bit. Let's think about it and talk about it sometime later."

Jimmy says, "I agree."

CHAPTER 8

The following morning a meeting was organized at the Ronald Reagan Building in downtown Washington, DC. The meeting was chaired by FBI Agent Haas; Nate and Bill, the two FBI agents who were at the NYC restaurant, were present; Mr. Smith from the CIA, and Major Pflueger from the Department of Defense were also there.

Haas states, "Please, everybody sit down. We have two agents up at Phillip's laboratory in New York State. We will contact them live. Those agents are also wearing body cams. Everything from the agents' cameras will be seen on a large screen on the wall in the conference room. Let's reach them," Haas says.

He pushes some buttons and immediately one of the two agents say, "Hello, Agent Haas."

"Hello," Haas responds. "Are you at the lab?"

The agent responds, "We think so."

"What do you mean you 'think so'?" Haas asks.

The second agent speaks up and says, "We just turned the corner on the path along the stream into the area where the entrance to the lab was located last week and there is nothing there."

Incredulously, Haas asks, "Are you just lost?"

The agent says, "No. We are verified by GPS. This is the site. There is nothing here except a hole in the side of the mountain where his lab was when we were here last."

Major Pflueger asks, "Was the lab blown up? Or burned down?"

The second agent answers, "Neither. It has simply disappeared."

Major Pflueger states, "There must be some debris present. Something left on the ground or in the bushes."

"There is only a hole in the side of the mountain where the lab used to be. But you are not going to believe this because the lab that we visited was about seventy yards by thirty yards. It extended from the mountain by about twenty yards. The mountain is granite," the second agent states. That agent continues, "The defect in the mountain has to be sixty yards high and eighty yards across and it goes back into the mountain about 300 yards in depth."

Mr. Smith tells them, "Go into the defect and determine, specifically, why the hole exists."

The second agent then says, "We have flashlights and we can see from out here into the defect, but I don't think we should go in there until we have some hazard suits. We didn't bring them along on this trip. We were not expecting this."

Mr. Smith then said, "We'll will contact the hazard team."

The agent responds, "Jack did that within moments of seeing what we are seeing right now."

The onsite first agent then said, "Even with a flashlight I cannot be certain how far back it goes. We're guessing 300 yards. I don't understand what I'm looking at because it doesn't look as if it was drilled out, hacked out, or blown out."

The second onsite agent then states, "There is a definite metallic odor as you get close to the opening. It keeps getting more noticeable the closer you get to the defect."

Everybody sitting at the table kept looking at each other silently hoping that one of the others could explain what they are hearing. Everyone was quiet.

Mr. Smith then says, "Are you sure that there are no signs of any burn marks of any kind?"

One onsite agent says, "Absolutely nothing that I can see."

Mr. Smith then says, "Head back to your car and wait for the arrival of the hazard team. Call us as they begin their tests."

The second onsite agent, confirms, "Will do."

CHAPTER 9

Jimmy and Melinda are in the kitchen staring out the back windows of the house into the yard where the two young girls are playing.

Jimmy writes on a paper towel: *You're the only person other than Mark who I ever spoke to about that drive from my home to Cambridge eleven years ago. This entire situation that is developing is directly related to that day.*

Melinda pauses then writes: *I would think about that story that you told me occasionally. I didn't want to fully believe what you saw that day. I did, however, believe you. I couldn't be sure, one way or another, that what my brain was telling me was true or not true. It was perplexing and that is probably the reason I've never brought it up with you before. It's crazy, isn't it? I knew that you were thinking about it, yet, I knew that you were not ready to talk about what you saw.*

Jimmy then writes: *You know, it was almost like a nightmare to me. The farther I got from that day the more time I spent trying to convince myself that it never happened.*

Melinda writes: *I understand.*

Jimmy then writes: *That day was totally confusing about everything after I saw that object but there was nothing confusing to me about leaving home and arriving at that point where I saw what I saw. There was no con-fusion about that part of what happened.*

"Did you ever try to draw it?" Melinda asked.

"Mark said to me that day when I got back to apartment that I should take a moment now and draw it in my head so I would never forget anything. Don't draw on paper. Don't draw it on the computer. Draw it in your brain," Jimmy whispered.

Jimmy went over to the radio and turned it on in high volume, then continued, saying, "There were hundreds of so-called 'spottings' around the country through that summer and fall. Before I saw what I saw I didn't believe people were seeing anything. After I saw what I saw, I knew that it was a UFO, but I didn't ever think that there were visitors from somewhere other than this planet. I thought it was military… our military."

Melinda asks, "Why did Mark think differently?"

Jimmy whispers, "This may sound odd, but the one question he kept asking me that day over and over again was about the object disappearing and reappearing."

"When I would hear or read about someone seeing what they called a UFO," Melinda says, "I actually can remember that many of them also described the disappearance and reappearance."

"You're absolutely right. What Mark briefly explained to me in the restaurant the other night drove that home. Why would it disappear and within microseconds appear at a distance from where it had been?" He continued, adding, "That is what he was fascinated by because everything else that I saw was just structural. Something disappearing is not structural. In order to disappear there has to be a place where it goes to and that place is unable to be seen. If you are able to determine where that place is, then you are back to the structural part of how to get there."

Melinda asks, "He said that he would send you all of his work. Is that correct?"

Jimmy says, "Yes and he emphasized that it would have every little portion of how he got to where he is today. He also, oddly enough, whispered that he will be explaining where he thinks everything will be going to in the future."

"Are you sure that the two people in that restaurant were trying to listen to your conversation?" Melinda asks.

Jimmy says, "I certainly think so. In all the confusion when Mark suddenly got up from the table when the sound of the glass or dish breaking occurred. Mark moved quickly toward the door of the restaurant, but I saw him drop a piece of paper off on a table where the two men were seated. They were looking at the area where the waiter or busboy dropped the dish. When they turned back, they saw the note. They looked at my table. They turned toward the door and saw Mark heading out. One of them quickly got up to follow him. The other was staring at me. I have no idea who they are."

Melinda whispers, "We have to be extremely careful as to who we talk to about this entire… whatever it is. We will have to talk, but we must only talk to people we trust."

Jimmy says, "I agree."

CHAPTER 10

The next meeting of the US intelligence group assigned to investigating what exactly was heard by the agents of the FBI at the restaurant in New York City convened. It was, once again, held at the Ronald Reagan Building in Washington, DC. The meeting was attended by Mr. Smith from the CIA, Agent Haas and his two fellow FBI agents, Bill and Nathan, and Major Pflueger from the Department of Defense. An agent, Andrew Rye, from the National Security Agency was present this time as well.

Michael begins the meeting stating, "At this time we need to keep this meeting small because we're missing a tremendous amount of information." He then pointed to the large flat television screen on the wall and said, "In a few minutes, we will be connected live to the laboratory site up north."

He turned to the FBI agents Bill and Nathan and asked, "Have you found any contact between O'Donnell and Loftus?"

Nathan answers, "We have everything possible covered. All phones, computers, laptops, iPads are under surveillance. The house is under observation twenty-four hours a day. We are using distance sound capture devices if he is talking to anybody outside. We have not been able to get inside his house yet so we cannot guarantee the ability to listen to every conversation inside his home. As soon as they leave their house for enough time, we will try to cover that as well. We can guarantee that ability for his work to be observed because that site is a part of the US Government. So far, we have found nothing. His friend Mark told him that he will have received all of the research and information on his project, but thus far we have not seen or heard anything that would make us think he has received it. We know what to look for in his daily activity if he is contacted."

Michael reaches toward the center of the table and hits a button on the central control device and a picture appears on the television screen. They were all looking at the defect in the side of the mountain where Mark O'Donnell's laboratory was once located. There appears to be at least 100 people in protection suits going in and out of a hole in the side of the mountain. They are carrying all types of devices used to study all surfaces. They were also studying the air inside and outside of the defect.

Suddenly one man walks up to the screen and says, "Morning, Mike. We've been at this since late yesterday afternoon. Samples of everything are being taken and sent to labs down in Washington. This is the craziest thing I've ever seen."

Michael asks him, "Is there anything left of the lab?"

The man says, "Absolutely nothing. Whatever was constructed here contained the lab and a lot more. We are talking about a large defect. So far, whatever was here must've been shaped something like a cigar. We're doing the laser photography so we'll have much more accurate information as to its shape. Those pictures will be ready later today. We'll be most accurate with that input in twenty-four hours."

Major Pflueger asks him, "Any traces of radiation?"

The man says, "We can detect some form of radiation but not dangerous levels. That part is very confusing. We need experts on fusion energy to look at this information because we think that fusion energy is more likely connected to this… to this laboratory than fission energy. We cannot be sure yet."

Agent Haas from the FBI asks the gentleman, "What do the walls look like?"

The man says, "This is going to sound odd, but they are moist. Moist rock. The other thing is that there is a definite odor of metal."

The agent then says, "I guess we have no answer yet, but we do have a lot of information to go through to try to understand something about this lab site and what really was constructed here. If your group does find anything important that may help us with our search up here, please notify us. Otherwise, I'll be back in touch with you tomorrow."

They all agreed.

Michael looks around the table and asks, "Does anybody have any other questions for now?"

Everybody shakes their heads.

He then says, "Each day let's start at 8:00 A.M. and go through some of this material that is sent down from the site. First, I am going to interview Dr. James Loftus."

CHAPTER 11

Jimmy and Melinda are having coffee and he is telling her about the scheduled meeting arranged at the Ronald Reagan Building.

He says, "The man from the FBI who I'll be meeting said that the meeting had to do with my routine evaluation since I'm dealing with more classified information than most government workers."

Melinda writes on a napkin: Did he mention Mark or the incident at the restaurant in New York?

Jimmy shakes his head and writes: *No. His request was brief. He confirmed the appointment with an email.*

Melinda whispers, "What do you think?"

Jimmy answers, "I'm sure that this meeting is specifically about... work." However, on the napkin he writes: *Mark and the restaurant.* And then verbally continues with, "And any information that I can give to them."

Melinda states, "Well, there is an awful lot that you can tell them because your work is expansive." Of course, the look on her face was quizzical.

Jimmy responds, "That's about it. So, I'm going to the meeting. but I won't be calling you afterward. We'll talk about it when I get home from work. Is that okay?"

Melinda answers, "Absolutely fine."

Jimmy finishes his coffee, washes the cup out, puts it in the sink, grabs his keys and heads out to his car. As is always the case in Washington, DC, a trip that should take you five minutes can easily take an hour. They have a little traffic problem. He is thinking to himself, *Wouldn't it be wonderful if I woke up next Monday morning and found that the Capitol of the United States of America was moved from Washington, DC to the middle of Kansas? It would be a pleasure driving to work.*

He arrived at the FBI Building and pulled his car into the parking lot about two blocks from the site. They had told him that he could park in the FBI Building's parking lot and he said Thank you, but he had no intention of parking in their lot. He walks the two blocks to the building. He goes through the front doors and then through the detection devices. He then takes the elevator to the eighth floor. He finds Agent Haas's office. He enters and greets the secretary at the front desk. He identifies himself. She smiles and says, "Agent Haas will see you now. Please follow me."

She walks about twenty yards down the corridor and opens the door to a conference room. No one was there. There is a large rectangular table with numerous seats and she says, "Sit anywhere you wish. Agent Haas will be here in a few minutes." Jimmy sits at the head of the table. The door opens and in walks Agent Haas. He is a slim gentleman about five foot eleven. His black hair combed straight back. He's wearing the classic perfectly fitting charcoal suit that is common to the FBI. The agents are well-dressed. That's the first difference between FBI agents and other agents. Jimmy always smiles at this because one that fits this description are the agents from the CIA who are not well-dressed.

Jimmy stands up as Agent Haas introduces himself. Jimmy shakes his hand and both sit down.

Haas then asks, "The reason that we're meeting has to do with your five- to ten-year evaluation regarding your intelligence access. This evaluation, actually, began a couple of weeks ago. It is mostly paper-work. There is nothing that we found that brought any concerns until a couple of nights ago. The two agents who were assigned to you for your fifth year evaluation were, as I suspect you know now, at the restaurant in New York City where you had dinner two nights ago. Our interests are not concerned about what happened from your standpoint. It has to do with your friend, Dr. Mark O'Donnell."

Jimmy interjects, "You know I hadn't seen Mark in over ten years. Not only had I not seen him, but I've not spoken to him. I've not heard from him in any manner until that night."

Haas pauses then asks, "Why is that?"

Jimmy says, "I have no idea. There was no argument between us. I did try to find him for years after graduation from MIT. I was unsuccessful. Initially I searched and wrote to mutual friends, but as years passed by, I didn't look anymore. I just didn't understand why I couldn't find him because we were good friends."

Haas asks, "No letters, no emails, no texts, no messages from other friends?"

Jimmy answers, "Nothing."

Haas asks, "Did you ever wonder what Dr. O'Donnell was doing?"

Jimmy states, "All the time."

Haas asks, "He graduated with the same degree as you?"

Jimmy states, "Yes, you already know that, the year before I did."

Haas then asks, "Did you know where he has been over the years since his graduation?"

Jimmy answers, "I heard that he went out to Cal Tech and got his doctorate. The degree was in astrophysics. I'm not sure where he went then. To be honest with you, it's more common for college friends to disappear from one another's lives than it is for high school friends to do the same."

Haas asks, "What do you know about Dr. O'Donnell economically?"

Jimmy smiles and says, "Mark's family was well off and he was the only child. I do know that his parents passed away and so I assume Mark inherited the estate."

Haas then asks, "Was he good at managing his own economics?"

Jimmy smiles again and says, "To be honest with you, I really don't think he cared about that."

Haas then asks Jimmy, "What exactly happened that night at the restaurant?"

Jimmy just recites exactly what he saw happen. What they spoke about and how the night abruptly ended.

Haas then asks, "The two agents there thought that they heard him talk about the ability to travel at a speed far beyond the speed of light. Is that true?"

Jimmy says, "That is what he said. To be specific far beyond the speed of light is what he… suggested."

Haas asks, "Did he say anything about the specifics of attaining that speed?"

Jimmy responds, saying, "He didn't say anything specific about it. All he did was show me a small vial of liquids. He said the answer is in there."

Haas pushes, asking, "Did you understand what he was telling you?"

Jimmy answered, "Not a clue. He simply told me that all information pertaining to that will be given to me. I have received nothing so far."

Haas then asks, "If you did receive information from him would you turn it over to us?"

Jimmy then says, "I would have no problem turning anything over to you, but I would have to contact my attorney first. This is Washington, DC. It is not the middle of Kansas. I have to be sure of my protection."

Haas then asks, "The agents at the restaurant weren't sure, but they thought that you were talking about UFOs. Is that true?"

Jimmy hesitates for a second and then said, "Our degrees are from MIT in astrophysics. UFOs are always talked about."

Haas then says, "And you spoke nothing more about that?"

Jimmy answers, "I mentioned or actually questioned him if UFOs are a part of this? He told me 'That doesn't matter.' I think your agents will tell you that the conversation was cut short."

Haas then asks, "Why was your conversation cut short?"

Jimmy says, "Well, it had nothing to do with me. I wanted to talk to him for hours when he appeared. Whatever happened I suspect only had to do with Mark and your agents. What happened, why it happened I have no idea."

Haas then asks, "If you hear from Dr. O'Donnell will you let us know?"

Jimmy quickly states, "Yes."

Jimmy then adds, "I'm assuming your agents at that restaurant and you have been doing a lot of research into Mark and me. Is that correct?"

Haas then says, "Yes. You're intelligent. I would expect you to know that is one of the purposes of our, your, government."

Jimmy asks, "You must answer me truthfully. It has been a couple of days since that evening at the restaurant in New York City. I'm assuming that you have been doing a lot of work investigating Mark, my wife, me, and probably even my little daughter. Is that correct?"

Haas answers yes.

Jimmy then says, "This is where I need you to be 100% truthful with me. Have you or anyone else involved in your investigation found anything showing that I have received any information?"

Haas answers, "No. We've found nothing."

That was the end of their meeting. They shook hands. Jimmy headed down to his car. He got in and just sat there staring out the front windshield focusing on nothing but mentally trying to explain what was going on with Mark and why the government is so secretive about their investigation. After about ten minutes, he started his car then headed off to work.

It is always the same situation in Washington, DC. It takes far too much time driving through the city. He eventually ended up at his office, which is located just behind the Capitol. He pulled into the lot, parked his car, got out, and headed up to his office. He chatted with several other people in his department and then asked his secretary if there were any messages.

She smiled and said, "Oh, Dr. Loftus, you know there are always messages but important messages? No, nothing important."

He was trying to get some work done, but his mind was fixated on everything that Mark said to him that evening in the restaurant.

One of his coworkers Larry Martin poked his head into Jimmy's office and said, "Is everything okay?"

Jimmy asked, "Why do you ask?"

Larry then said, "Well, because every secretary and everybody who has seen you today thought you looked a bit pale. Physically you're okay right?"

Jimmy answered, "Physically I'm sure I'm okay."

Larry then asked, "Everything okay at home?"

Jimmy said, "Everything is fine at home. Someday this week you and I will talk about this. Is that okay?"

Larry said, "Talking is always good. We must never keep secrets and a lot of the time the answer to what you may be looking for is something you already knew. I'll catch you later."

Jimmy said, "Thanks, Larry."

Chapter 12

Jimmy went to his private office. He was trying as hard as he could to work on numbers related to the current program that he was involved in at work. In that project was trying to find some way to understand the interaction between dark energy and dark matter. The project has scientists from numerous countries involved. Scientists always believe there is an answer to every problem. Oddly enough, his mind kept coming back to what Larry had just said to him. He may be staring the answer right in the face. So often when a scientist is asked how does dark matter or dark energy work or even what they actually are, the answer is "We just do not know."

The paper that he was working on that day was not working out numerically. He took the paper, crushed it into a ball, and was about to throw it into the garbage can, but it slipped from his hand and fell on the floor under the desk.

Jimmy said in frustration, "Great."

He pushed his chair back and got down on his knees to reach underneath his desk. He got the paper and he was moving back away from his desk when he suddenly stopped. He stood up and said nothing. He suddenly realized that he might know exactly where the information that Mark had said he would receive actually was. What he was missing since that time in the restaurant was what Mark actually said: *"You will have received the information."* Mark was actually telling him that he had gotten the information to him before the meeting at the restaurant!

Mark quickly got up from his desk and was about to reach for his phone to call his wife, but then he hesitated, realizing that most likely all of his phones were tapped. That also meant he could not even send her an email or text.

He went down the hall to Larry's office and stuck his head in and said, "You know I think I meant to go home and take a rest. That's okay with you, right?"

Larry said, "No problem. I'll see you tomorrow or whenever. Just get some rest."

Jimmy said, "Thanks."

He then went down to the parking lot, got his car, and started his drive back to his home. He drove slowly and decided to make an excuse as to why he left work. He stopped at a pharmacy on Connecticut Avenue to purchase some cold pills. He then went to a grocery store across the street and purchased some items for the house. Then he slowly drove home.

Chapter 13

Jimmy arrived at his house and parked his car outside of his garage, which is behind the backyard. He got out of his car went through the back gate into the garden and into the back of the house. He continued into the kitchen where he found his wife, Melinda, what she refers to as "sorting." It is, actually, excellent organization. When she saw him, her eyes opened wide telling him two things. First, she was happy to see him and second why was he here so early?

She asks, "Why—?"

Jimmy brought his right thumb and index finger up to his lips and made the motion of zipping his mouth shut. She knew what he meant.

Jimmy then says, "I was just tired at work today. I decided to come home. Maybe I'm getting a cold. I picked up some pills just in case. Got some soda as well. You already know that I had a meeting with Agent Haas this morning at the FBI. He had nothing new regarding this whole situation." Jimmy zips his mouth again.

Melinda says, "Oh well."

There was a napkin on the cutting table located in the center of their kitchen. Jimmy had gotten his pen out and wrote on the napkin: I know where it is!

Melinda tilts her head with an expression of question on her face.

Jimmy writes on the napkin: *the information.*

Her eyes open wide followed by a smile.

Melinda then said, "Well, help me sort out this cabinet and then we can sit down and watch some TV or find some other chore."

Jimmy says, "Fine but let me get out of these work clothes."

Melinda laughs out loud and asks, "Work clothes?"

He goes up to the bedroom and removes his suit and shirt and socks and shoes. Hangs them up and gets a pair of jeans and a sweatshirt and puts on a pair of athletic socks. He grabs his sneakers and carries them down the steps and as he passes the room that they call their office he tosses the sneakers into that room.

When he gets back into the kitchen he asks Melinda "Have you seen my sneakers?"

She looks at him quizzically.

He then says, "Oh that's right I left them in our office."

He then walks down the hall into their office and one sneaker was on the edge of their rather large desk and the other, thank God, was under the desk. He got down on his knees he crawled under the front of the desk and there it was. The sneaker was there, of course. However, as he scans the underside of his desk he finds, right in front of him, stuck to the underside of his desk with a piece of Nora's bubblegum a small container of computer chips. He gently pries it loose and puts it in his pocket all while he was still under the desk. He grabbed his sneaker went over to one of the side chairs and put them on and he walked back into the kitchen. He had a smile on his face and Melinda's eyes were wider than when he came in the back door. Jimmy was giving her the thumbs-up.

Melinda says, "You know, Jimmy, I think both you and I need some time away from the city. We can go down to the beach for a long week-end."

They were family owners in a four-bedroom home on the Atlantic Ocean in Virginia.

Jimmy paused and then said, "What a great idea! My sister is somewhere off in California for the summer so she won't be down there. Let's invite David and Lynn Cox and see if they'd like to get away for a weekend. One thing I do know is David likes to fish."

Melinda had written on another napkin: *I'll go ask them and I'm going to ask Lynn to pick up a new laptop and that we'll reimburse her.* Jimmy nodded.

Jimmy said, "Why don't you drop over to their house and ask them."

Melinda said, "I'm on my way, but let me call them first to see if they're at home."

She picked up the phone and called the Cox's number. Lynn answered and Melinda began to tell her why she's calling and if they would be interested. Then Melinda told her, "Let me come over to your house and I'll explain where it is and when we all could be going down." Lynn then said that they have access to a home in Ocean City, Maryland and that would be closer. Melinda listens for a little bit and then she said, "Great I'll be right over."

She looked at Jimmy and they then nodded at each other but kept quiet.

CHAPTER 14

On Thursday morning Melinda, Jimmy, and Lily were in their car packed and heading toward the Virginia coast. The Cox family would be leaving about an hour later and Melinda had given them the exact coordinates on GPS for the location of the house. They were on route US 50 heading to the Chesapeake Bay Bridge. They had all discussed which house to go to and agreed that Ocean City would be closer. But though they said they were going to Ocean City, they were not. It is Thursday morning and the traffic crossing that bridge is significantly reduced. During the summer months traveling this route any Friday or Saturday is stop and go for miles if you are traveling east. On Sunday it has the same congestion traveling west.

The house in Virginia sits right behind the sand dunes on the beach. The closest houses to it would be about 200 yards north and south. There are no houses or other structures on the bay side. The road behind the house is a sand and gravel road that comes in off the winding dune road. In the back of the house there are sand dunes mixed with sea oats and cactus. These dunes are small. The largest ones may be a foot in height. If you sat on any of the decks that surround the house your view is spectacular. In the evening you can see all the way from the ocean and the beaches through the dunes and all of the way westward to the bay area. If the sky is clear you are able to see beautiful sunsets on the bay.

After about four hours on the road they reached the beach home.

As they drove up to the house, Melinda told her daughter "Do not ever go to the beach unless your dad or I or one of Nora's parents are with you. You understand, don't you?"

Her daughter jokingly answered, "Yes, Mommy!"

Melinda said again, "I'm serious about this. Do you promise me?"

Her daughter said, "Yes."

Melinda then said, "Well, let's start unpacking."

They had stopped in the town of Princess Anne as they drove down Route 13 through Maryland heading to Virginia and went to a grocery store. They purchased all of the essential foods for breakfast, lunch, and dinner. There is a small but limited store about ten miles away from their house, and they could always shop there if they ran out of anything essential.

The skies are blue and the temperatures is 80°F. After finishing unpacking their luggage and other items, Jimmy stands out on the deck facing the ocean for a couple minutes and thought, as most people do, about the attraction that people have for the ocean. There have been thousands of explanations, but the only one that truly made sense is that the ocean is where the human beings came from initially. It is connected to the human past. It was their original cave.

Jimmy does not have a computer in the house and he did not bring one with him. Unknown to the people who would be interested if he had a computer with him, Lynn Cox is carrying a new unopened laptop and, hopefully, they were never investigating Lynn. Yet, those same people think that the Coxes and the Loftuses were heading to Ocean City, Maryland. All talk designated that it was that home where they would be spending the weekend.

About an hour after the Loftus group reached Virginia, the Cox family arrived. Melinda and Jimmy went outside to greet them. Dave was saying how the drive went quite well and they all began bringing in their packed items.

The house is a four-bedroom and has two master bedrooms, one normal bedroom and one bedroom with bunkbeds for the kids.

As soon as they were all unpacked and settled into their rooms Lynn said, "I don't know about you, but I mean to head down to the beach and just relax."

Everybody vehemently agreed. They carried their beach chairs and a small cooler for their water and beer.

Jimmy asked David, "Are you going to fish in the surf?"

David responded, "Not now. When you fish the ocean, you fish the tides. Now it's an outgoing tide. Maybe this evening."

Jimmy answered, "Hope that you can improve my surf fishing."

He was explaining to Melinda and Jimmy that the fish that can be caught in this particular area are flounder, sea trout, blue fish, and anything wandering up from the south. He did not tell them that sharks are easy to catch as well. The sharks, however, only come in at evening time and nighttime. They come in from the ocean to feed. He will remember to tell everybody about the increased danger of going into the ocean later in the day.

Carrying their beach chairs, umbrella, towels and the cooler for water and beer they made their way down to the edge of the ocean and planted themselves in the sand and just relaxed. They soaked up the sun for a few hours and then headed back up to the house to make dinner.

After dinner, as the sun began to set, they headed back down to the beach. On the eastern United States beaches, the sun sets behind you. Objects that were hidden by the sunlight slowly begin to appear in the sky. About one half hour after full sunset and if the sky is not blocked by clouds, you find yourself staring at the majesty of the Milky Way.

They all sat silently staring at the sky and listening to the waves pouring on to the beach. The little girls were off to the side laughing, whispering, and digging a hole in the sand.

After a few minutes Lynn then asked, "Does it scare you? I mean does the sky scare you?"

Everyone is silent for a little bit. Each is thinking that they had never thought of the night sky being frightening.

Melinda then answers, "No, it doesn't."

The men are quiet. Lynn then says, "I find the night sky comforting. It's inviting. Odd, isn't it?"

Her husband David then says, "I never thought of that. Here I am sitting on a beach looking up into a clear night sky. Peering at the Milky Way and I find it so comforting. To be honest with you, I know very little about our galaxy let alone the entire universe. My profession has always been concentrated here on Earth. However, we have to deal with objects, meteors, that landed on Earth from far out in the universe."

Jimmy says, "Believe me, David, no one knows very much about our galaxy or the universe. As our scopes and detection devices become more sensitive, we learn but what we learn compared to the actual facts is very little."

David says, "Well, in any case, looking at it brings me comfort."

Jimmy whispers, "Agreed."

Lynn then explains, "Several years ago I began to try to understand why it would bring me comfort. After many nights, I came to understand that it was the light in the sky. I ignored the darkness, but I was fixated on the light."

Melinda asks, "Did it feel as if the light was calling to you?"

Lynn answers, "Yes. Calling me. This may sound odd, but I felt I was part of that light. It is as if I am looking at my entire family from a distance, but we see each other extremely clearly. Everyone is smiling. Strange, isn't it?"

Jimmy says, "What we see is what my profession tries to understand. We know so little. Things that in the past were said to be impossible are now accepted as truth. At least some think it is truth and even that may change again. Many people think that astrophysics is a huge ocean of information that we dip into in order to answer questions. But I will tell you that is not the case. It is not a deep ocean of knowledge. It is more like an active volcano that is spewing out new ideas, new facts, new questions every second. Just like volcanic lava it rolls down the side of the volcano and as it cools it hardens. In other words, what came out may hardened into accepted truth but it was not. That is one of the things that I do. I try to distinguish the truth from the untruth and if the untruth has hardened into rock it is difficult to get people, even myself, to pry it loose and let the truth replace it."

Everyone is quiet for a moment and then Jimmy adds, "Looking at the sky and feeling comfort is a lot more important than looking at the sky and feeling questions. Tonight, I feel comfort."

Melinda then says, "Yes. For tonight comfort. Lynn is correct. It is as if that light in its thousands or millions or trillions of points is calling to me. The light and I are the same. We are both energy."

They sat for a few more minutes and then they all got up and headed from the beach, up the dune and back toward the house.

They had prearranged never to talk about what was about to happen in the house at any time before that moment. They knew they were under surveillance and having the investigators follow the path of them getting away for some rest was important. Where they are at this time is probably the safest place to be.

CHAPTER 15

They went back into the house and kept their conversation concentrated on how relaxing it is being at the beach. They never mentioned the chips or the laptop. They watched TV for about an hour. The children were asked to head off to bed. They then sat down in the living room on an L-shaped sofa and Lynn got the laptop out of her luggage and put it on the coffee table in front of the four.

Jimmy handed her the chip and she put it into the computer. No one said a word. The small laptop is not online. They will only watch the chip and keep the computer volume as well as their speaking volume low.

Mark's image appeared on the screen. He was smiling.

He began, "Hello, Jimmy. I'm going to assume I'm looking at you and I'll be hoping that Melinda, Lynn, and David are there as well. At least that's how it should be. That is how Paul, Patty, Emmy, and I planned it." He continued, explaining, "On this chip you will find everything from the start to the end of my journey. On the second chip you will find all of the technical information as to how and why a vehicle must be constructed in a certain manner. Any country, any group can be assured that they always have the option of actually traveling enormous distances in this universe. On that fall day in Cambridge I

67

promised you that I would eventually be able to explain to you what you saw. I eventually did unravel it, but most interesting was what I determined why they were here.

"It is that information that is most important. Remember this. What we'll be talking about goes far beyond Earth, far beyond humans, far beyond other beings, far beyond all matter and all energy. It is this that will be so important that we do not allow any government to be the sole possessor of this information. It must be shared throughout the world but not by governments. Each government will receive the second chip but so will each person. How we'll do this, I'll explain later."

Jimmy hit the Pause button and once again explained that day when he drove from his home in Williams, Massachusetts to Cambridge. He went into detail as to what he saw. He explained how it affected him mentally as he tried to see as much of the vessel as possible. He tried to describe how the rest of his drive back to Cambridge was extremely difficult because his mind was in a thousand different places.

He went on to describe the meeting with Mark when he arrived at their house in Cambridge. He told them that Mark kept asking certain questions over and over again. Jimmy explained how Mark was most interested in my description of the vessel disappearing and immediately reappearing in a different place. The position of the vessel varied. Sometimes only twenty yards higher when it reappeared. Other times 100 yards off to the side. Then it would disappear and reappear somewhere else again. He explained how Mark kept asking him if he was sure that it was disappearing and not moving at a speed so fast that his eyes could not determine the difference.

Jimmy said, "I just could not say with certainty it was one or the other." He then hit the Play button and Mark continued.

"What you described to me was something that I would have doubted if I did not hear it from you. However, I heard it from you and that alone made me believe that it was true. That's the reason for the secrecy. If this entire event were discussed out in the open, most scientists would have doubted it. We all know that scientific research into something of this nature would not occur. That is, unless its existence is proven first. A group, community or country may believe that science is science and fantasy is fantasy. What scientists do not understand causes them to deny the existence of the subject and they would block any research. Here is where science and fantasy cross paths. So, I did my own research. I did it under a different name simply to not allow anything to interfere with my work.

"After you told me what you experienced on that fall day I knew that at least some of the descriptions of possible UFOs through time all around the earth were real. Obviously, what I did not know was the origin of the vessels nor why they were here. So, I began researching information on all of the reports by people all around the globe and tried to see if any of the descriptions matched your description.

"Actually, many of the reports did match. The part that was especially common was the disappearance and reappearance of the object. This is what captured me more than anything else. It was extremely interesting to see the numerous shapes that were reported. Many were triangular but many were not. The speed described in each case was unexplainable based on our current knowledge of producing speed.

"Therefore, where I began was with the disappearance and reappearance. I was trying to figure out if the vessel had really disappeared or whether it just moved at a speed that our eyes were not capable of registering. The answer was they were both true. They did actually have the capability of disappearing and they could travel at speeds far beyond anything we could ever imagine. I know that you are thinking how can that be?

"If you read through modern-day science you will see hundreds of new methods to increase speed. You will also find hundreds of new methods to create disappearance. None of them could ever match what you saw. So, I asked the question as to whether there is something discussed in science that absolutely no one can explain? You know that there is such a thing, right, Jimmy?

Jimmy whispers to everyone, "Dark matter and dark energy."

Mark continued and said that it was the dark matter and dark energy that even the best scientists alive cannot begin to explain. He explained, "The Scientific Community believes that dark matter and dark energy are real, but they cannot explain it. On telescopes they have seen galaxies surrounded by dark matter and dark energy colliding with other galaxies that were also surrounded by dark matter and dark energy. The galaxies show signs of collision, but the dark matter and dark energy would just go through the collision as if it never happened. I will explain to you later the similarity of this collision that we see through telescopes and the mystery particle called neutrino that by the billions run right through our bodies and through the Earth and science cannot physically detect it.

"We believe trillions of particles stream through the Earth, but we have problems possibly identifying one particle. The only thing we do know about this dark universe is that it can affect our universe only by its presence. Dark matter and dark energy are something totally separate from us. They are part of a different universe and I believe at some point billions of years ago a small part of our universe broke into the universe of dark matter and energy. That is when time started. There is no time until you have at least two objects totally different from each other. One versus the other is measured as time. I personally think that the mixing of two different universes was the Big Bang.

"What we were prior to the breakthrough was pure plasma in our own universe. As that plasma poured into the dark universe the dark universe began to try to contain the invader. How they did it is interesting. Think of it this way. Imagine the snow falling and the snow is us. In the same way that we go out to clear the snow, there are basically three methods. One method is to shovel it into a pile. This is what I believe dark matter did and still does. It led eventually to the formation of hydrogen because this original plasma had to find a way to protect itself. Later stars formed and even later galaxies.

"The next method of dealing with the snow is using a broom and spreading it around. This is what I believe dark energy does and this is the greatest risk to us, to our solar systems, to the stars, to our galaxies, to our universe. This is something that our Scientific Community does believe. We have proven that everything in the universe that we see is rapidly moving away from everything else. It is just like being swept by the broom. Science knows that eventually the distance between each object will be so far that it will disappear. What the dark universe did not expect is that our universe plasma holds on to itself. Rather that moving two pieces of plasma away from each other it acts more like taffy. As you grab each end of a piece of taffy and spread it apart it stays connected no matter how far apart you spread. Just like Einstein's riddle. However, the dark universe thinks it will snap. I suspect it will snap.

"The third method is to melt the snow. This is what we know as 'black holes.' That is what we face. That is the end. You can kill matter, but you cannot kill energy and that energy may just change into matter because it needs other energy to stay as energy. If everything is swept away from everything, we will be lost forever. This is the greatest threat to us and, yes, to other beings. There are many other things that can, at any time, eliminate this planet where we live. Gamma rays from star explosions, blackhole explosions, magnetars, and others could destroy this planet if we were sitting in the path of that energy. I am sure the earth was in the path of one beam of energy from a magnetar many times in the past. It may have caused the extinction of living things on this planet numerous times.

"The earth was hit in 2004 by a beam from a magnetar. If you ask people if they knew that had happened they would answer that they never heard of this event occurring. But it did happen and the beam came from the other side of our galaxy and it did damage to the atmosphere of our planet. At some point in our life each of us must ask what we are doing here on Earth? I think this explains it. However, it is only part of the story. Our plasma is in many forms in our universe. It is you, me, the sun, the earth, rocks, water, air, stars. It wants to go home. Everything that people have been seeing in the skies and even down on Earth that we call UFOs are actually beings who want to go home. I will explain this in more detail to you later. They are all heading home. They are not planning to invade the Earth. We are a gas station like the one that I spoke to you about in Williamsport, Pennsylvania. I will show you something that will begin to explain how everything is possible. What I will show you is within that little bottle."

Jimmy pauses the chip and whispers, "In the restaurant he pulled out a little bottle that he held up for me to see and what I was looking at was a bottle of water and oil and you can see the oil is floating on top of the water. There was no mixture of the two. Then he shook it and it seemed as if everything was mixed but we know it wasn't. It can't mix. I believe that this is what he is talking about when he refers to our matter and our energy and dark matter and dark energy."

Jimmy restarted the chip.

Mark continued to explain that we know virtually nothing about dark matter and dark energy except that it exists. He goes on to say that it is not "dark." It is "clear." He said, "Imagine that it's like an Olympic-size swimming pool full of water and if you were on the edge of the pool talking to someone who is inside the pool the part of his body that is out of the pool is seen clearly. However, the part of his body that is underwater is distorted. If we got into the pool and the person was close by what we see is clearer. If we went underwater what we see is even more clear. Even if we went underwater to look at something and the water in the pool was completely still there was still some distortion. If the water, however, was disturbed we would not be able to see anything at all. The image would be so distorted that the person or object almost becomes invisible. This does not explain the disappearance of the vessels because they do not nor cannot enter the universe of dark matter or dark energy.

"However, Jimmy, the most important thing that we already know is that if you took that bottle that I showed you in the restaurant and you looked at the contact between the oil and the water you already know that there has to be a space between the two forms of liquid. This was taught to us in our first physics courses. There is a space and that space is the key to everything. The vessels were able to get into that space. You remember that video that was released from Chile that showed a UFO, don't you? The part of that video that had me captivated was the dark discharge behind the object. To be exact it was the fact that what I saw was that the discharge seemed to be contained in a tubelike object behind the UFO. The discharge extended quite a distance behind the object. We see trails in our atmosphere behind jets but very quickly they begin to dissipate or spread apart due to the winds. At times it seems to disappear when it crosses a significant temperature difference in the sky. In the Chilean video, the discharge seemed contained. It was as if the vessel was in a space different from everything around it.

"The more I looked at that video the more things began to fall into place. In that little bottle I showed you was water and oil and they do not mix. We have our matter and our energy and then there is the dark matter and the dark energy and they do not mix. It was the disappearance and reappearance of the crafts in UFO reports that had captivated me. It took me about two years to come to understand that they do not really disappear. They go somewhere else. They go into that 'In Between' space between our universe and the dark matter and dark energy universe."

"Once I had accepted that, I had to figure out how these vessels did it. That is where David comes in. I believe he could explain to you what I was searching for. He will tell you that we found it. Everything that you'll be reading on these chips does not come from me alone. There are numerous people from all aspects of life that I sat down with and discussed certain aspects of what we were dealing with at the time. Many of these people you will need to speak with as well. I suspect that you have already spoken to David and Lynn. What each person says to you is extremely important. Just listen to them. The large picture of what we're exploring was not talked about with anyone. Perhaps they have thought about it, but our discussions were concentrated on their part of solving the question. You will be the first to hear it and you will see that it expands far beyond anything you could ever imagine. It is that aspect that is going to need to be addressed, but how it is addressed and put forth is extremely important.

"Therefore, at this point I explained the disappearance and how it occurred. In my mind this verified completely that the UFOs truly exist. However, the entire picture was coming into focus and it did not seem to be anything close to what believers in UFOs thought."

Mark then looked directly into the camera and said, "Jimmy, you remember exactly what Tillie told you that day you left your hometown before crossing paths with the vessel don't you? Always remember this. It is important. What Tillie said to you is 100% accurate."

<h1 style="text-align:center">Chapter 16</h1>

They all agreed to turn the laptop off since it was getting late and each one of them had a tremendous amount to think about because of what they had just heard. They would get back to the chip the following day. During the next day they must never mention Dr. O'Donnell or the chip. It would be an intense night of whispering to one another because of the magnitude of what they have just heard and what they will be dealing with in the future. They believe that Mark has already worked out a plan to protect them. At this point, how that will be done is the question. They knew that they had to distribute the information outlined by Mark. They knew there will be huge numbers of people trying to stop that goal.

In the house they softly spoke to each other about normal subjects being sure to never mention the chip. Eventually, they headed off to their bedrooms and the dads stopped by their children's room to make sure the girls were okay. They said "good night" and headed off to their bedrooms.

It took a while for each of them to fall asleep. Before arriving at that degree of fatigue where you can no longer stay awake, each whispered questions to each other to which the answer was universally—"I do not know" or "I'm not sure."

They awoke the next morning and each headed down to the kitchen area where Jimmy had been up earlier and made a pot of coffee. He was putting out some scones on a large plate. He used that fabulous recipe that his coworker Joy taught him. He had cereal, bowls, glasses and spoons ready for the kids. When Melinda, Lynn, and David smelled the coffee, it must have been like someone telling them to get up. Prior to being ensconced in the smell of freshly made coffee, lingering sleep kept telling you *"there's no reason to get up."* That all changes with one whiff.

Jimmy was sitting out on the deck facing the ocean. The day was beautiful. There were no clouds in the sky. The sun had been up for about an hour. Everybody had their coffee and grabbed a chair and sat down. Jimmy was staring straight out to sea. When they arrived at the kitchen he said, "Good morning, did you sleep well?" Each one of them answered the exact same way. Speaking "yes" as their heads sway side to side in "no." As they brought a mug of coffee near their upper lip even as they stared out to the sea each answering, "Oh, yes."

David then said to Jimmy, "The tide is coming in, I believe. When we go down to the beach, we can see if we can catch some fish for lunch or supper?"

Jimmy says, "Sounds great to me."

The women told them that they're going to go for a walk. After drinking their coffee and finishing their scones the men gathered their fishing equipment and headed down toward the surf. Melinda and Lynn headed the opposite direction toward the dunes. The children followed their dads.

At the beach David had brought down two medium-size surf rods and he and Jimmy had set up the lines and were fishing quite close to shore. David called it "flounder waters." On an incoming tide the flounder frequently may be sitting a foot off of the shoreline.

David said, "It was a day like this out on the beach on the Outer Banks of North Carolina where we first met him. I was surf fishing and

Lynn was sitting in her chair reading. Mark and his wife came strolling down the beach and they asked me if my fishing was going as planned?"

He continued. "Odd question, wasn't it? In reality the more years you fish the less you plan, and for some reason I felt that he understood that as soon as I heard the question. I have no idea why I felt that."

David continued. "We introduced ourselves and then we went back up onto the beach to where Lynn was sitting and introduced each other there again. During that week we would see each other rather frequently. They were extremely honest and friendly people."

Jimmy said, "I never met his wife, Patty, but I can guarantee you that you're feeling about Mark was correct."

David said, "They're like twins. And what do you think he asked me about?"

Jimmy said, "Metals."

David smiled and said, "Yes, eventually we drifted onto that subject. He acted surprised when he found out that I am a metallurgist. To this day I'm really not sure whether he was surprised or he knew before I ever met him. What he was interested in was certain metals that can become liquid at certain degrees. The metal had to be controlled in its liquid state. He wanted to be able to manipulate the metal to an extremely small point, like the point of an excessively sharp spear. He had told me that he had studied astrophysics at MIT but he did not exactly tell me why he was asking that question about the metal types. Obviously, now I know the importance of what he was asking me. I assume that he has been successful in creating or finding a way to bring the point of metal in a liquid state to make a small puncture in our side of the universe. Being a metallurgist, it makes sense because all you need is a small opening and things will flow through that opening. We talked at length about specific metals and especially about isotope ratios and isotope manipulation."

David continued. "At times I thought that he knew which of the metals he was most interested in, but he never mentioned which one it was. He would ask me in very detailed questions as to whether we have the equipment to change isotope ratios in a given metal."

Jimmy said, "I suspect we're going to find out which metal he chose."

David said, "Now this may sound odd, but it was as if someone told him which specific metal."

Jimmy asked, "Did you have answers when he asked?"

David paused and then said, "Yes. With the correct light, heat, chemicals, there are laboratories around the world that can change isotope ratios."

Jimmy then said, "We have recovered metals from outer space that do not exist here on this planet. They arrived as meteors and we have thought that they were constructed inside an exploding star. We assumed that."

David said, "That assumption may be true, but it may not be true."

Jimmy then says, "So, as far as I can understand your conversations with him, he was searching for a metal that can somehow open that space between our matter and dark matter. Do you agree?"

David said, "After last night, I agree. If I had never heard every aspect and I mean every aspect of this project I would never have thought that was the purpose of the metal."

Jimmy then whispers, "I think everything is going to get much more intricate… much more than anything we can ever imagine."

David responds, "Agreed," then adds, "I thought that I heard him whisper something when we were on the beach at night toward the end of the week. He was staring up into the sky and I thought I heard him whisper 'magnetic control.'"

CHAPTER 17

The rest of the day passed by quietly. It is funny how our minds may look at the same item over and over again and then see it so differently.

After supper the young girls were playing a card game on the dining room table and the four adults were out on the porch looking over the Atlantic Ocean.

Lynn quietly asked Jimmy, "I know that you're a very religious person."

Jimmy quickly responded, "Yes, I am a Catholic and my parents were Catholics and their parents were Catholics and their parents were Catholics. I have this strong feeling that my family were Catholics before Catholicism was a reality.

Lynn laughed and asked, "I guess what I'm asking is did any of this boardgame that we are learning affect your faith?"

Jimmy paused and then said, "No. From the very beginning and I mean beginning when I was a freshman at MIT studying astrophysics through the day when I saw what I saw on that road in western Massachusetts and up to this very moment when the reality of everything is beginning to become clear, my faith has only gotten stronger. In Catholicism you hear the phrase rather frequently 'the mystery of faith.'

The church never tells you that it is a sin to try to understand the mystery. They simply tell us that the important aspect is your faith and we must accept the mystery because the entire mystery may be unsolvable."

Lynn asks, "Why? Why can't we solve it?"

Jimmy says, "God is behind the mystery, Lynn, not you, not me, not David or Melinda, and not Mark. The number of people in my profession that I meet who are agnostics or atheists is quite high. They frequently ask me why do I have faith? I always answer them the same way. I tell them that if you took every grain of sand off every beach in the world and from the bottom of every ocean and lake and desert in the world and you made a huge pile of sand they should think that would be God and if I took one grain of sand from that pile that is what I would know about God and the mystery. I then tell them, if you are a priest or a rabbi or a minister, then you might get two grains."

Lynn smiles and says, "You're right. You have solved a little bit of the mystery."

Jimmy wonders very quietly, "I wonder what Mark is going to tell us tonight?"

As the evening moved on and after darkness had arrived they had the kids go to bed. Without speaking they brought out the laptop and put in the chip. They all sat close to each other on the couch with the laptop on the table in front of them. They begin exactly where they left off last night.

Mark began, "Jimmy, you know why I kept asking you about the vessel disappearing and reappearing. That was what spurred me on because in the world that we know, things can't disappear. If something is right in front of you, then you can see it. So, beginning on the night you told me about the vessel, my thoughts were entangled in whether what you described could move so fast that the human sight system could not keep up with it at extremely high speeds. This made more sense scientifically rather than it just disappeared. It took me awhile but

I finally came to understand that the answer was both. The vessel could move outrageously fast but it could also change where it existed.

"Dark matter and dark energy are real. Our matter and our energy are real. They are there and they are here. When we look out into the universe what we see is 86% dark matter and dark energy. As you know they were given the name dark not because they are dark. There were given that name because they were a mystery that no one could solve and to this day no one has solved except that they are there. That is what we must accept. So much of the research today is devoted to neutrinos. The mistake that they are making, I believe, is that they are assuming neutrinos are from the matter from our universe. I think you are beginning to understand what I am saying. We are dealing with two different universes and the key to everything is that you and I and every person and every bit of air and rock and energy and light are of our universe but not the dark universe. Just like in that little bottle I showed you in the restaurant where there is oil and water each passes the other with no apparent resistance. The neutrino may actually belong to the dark universe. They go through extensive structures and methods to try to capture a few of the neutrinos, but they have not been very successful.

"That is what I was trying to show you with that little bottle. The bottle contained oil and water and they simply do not mix, but as I had mentioned earlier, one can affect the other simply because it exists. There was a time when all the space that we are in now was pure dark matter and dark energy but, somehow, we came into that universe. I suspect that it was simply an inadvertent collision that momentarily opened the door and some of the contents of our universe came tumbling into this universe. What we must remember is everything is exactly as we saw in that little bottle.

"One thing I can tell you is that the dark matter and dark energy did not want us here. What has allowed us to stay in existence was the manner of which dark matter dealt with us. Many believe that at the beginning of our universe we were simply plasma formed by the 'Big Bang.' I suspect we were plasma but that form is what we were in our own universe. When dark matter began encircling us we fought for our existence. We formed stars and stars formed galaxies. The dark energy would no longer allow this to go on. It began to sweep. This is the desire of the dark energy. This is why the vessel you saw and all others like it exist. They do not know anything more about dark matter or dark energy than we do, but they do know as we have just determined what effect the dark universe will have upon us. They feel that we must get back to the starting point."

Mark pauses and then begins again. "I suspect that you will ask the question that everyone would ask: did you meet the people in the vessel? My answer is very important. Because it doesn't really matter whether I met with them or not. What is important is why they were here. The answer to the question is that they were heading somewhere and it was not here. Just like the description I gave to you as an example of someone leaving New York City to drive to Los Angeles and there on the road going across Pennsylvania. So, what do you expect to happen? All of the people in that area of Williamsport, like us, are going down to the gas station asking the owners who you were? Where are they from? Why were they here? You see, with the beings that we are talking about, they are going somewhere, and believe me it is not for a vacation. The most important thing to understand is exactly where they think they are going."

Mark continues, "As you know there are most likely hundreds of thousands of situations where people on this planet saw something in the sky or maybe on the ground. What they saw varies extensively. For some they saw a shadow. For others they saw a light. Many saw vessels. There are people who feel they saw the entities that were in control of the vessels. In most cases the exact nature of what these people saw can be explained by known physics. There were, however, thousands of occurrences that cannot be explained by known physics. You know this now, Jimmy, don't you? You could not explain what you saw.

"Therefore, Jimmy, that is where I began. I had to begin looking into each of these occurrences or sightings. What I was looking for was some consistency, some pattern in what was reported as being seen. This was essential. I had to know the description of what was seen, where it was seen, and all of the circumstances around the occurrence."

He continued. "This information was fascinating. The shape of the vessel when seen really came down to a very few forms. None of these forms matched what science fiction writers created. The vessels were pretty much rounded on the ends. Not like *Star Trek*, right, Jimmy? Sometimes they were shaped like a cigar. Other times like a Tic-Tac. Frequently they were Delta shaped, but even when people saw this shaped vessel if you listen to what they describe you will hear them all saying that it was 'rounded on the ends.' That is what you saw.

"So, the rounded edges were for some reason extremely important. You will see why. Remember what I mentioned about the fact that there is a space between our matter and energy and the dark matter and energy. These vessels were able to get into that space and travel and the rounded structure suddenly becomes understandable.

"Obviously I had to find out how they were able to get into that space. You saw the vessel up close. You knew it was some form of metal. One thing for sure is that form of metal may not be found on this planet. I am not saying that it is not here or that it could not be created here. I am saying that no one knows about it. It is for this reason that I began searching to find it. One thing for sure that I can tell you is that if it was not here, then the vessels would not be here either.

"They came to Earth by traveling in the 'In Between' space. A space where we suspect there is no gravity. If you look at projected maps of Dark Matter/Energy connecting to Earth they look like Earth with dark areas surrounding and going into the Earth. The vessels will be seen or not seen depending upon the curves and depths of the 'In Between.'

"So you can see why the location of people sightings of vessels was so important. Remember that this is like a trip from New York City to

Los Angeles and you wouldn't stop at a Lumber Store to get gas for your car. All of the information on these sightings and where they have been possibly seen are in the footnotes on this chip. You will see that certain areas keep repeating far too frequently. Those sites would be volcanoes, rocky desert areas, deep lakes and oceans. The lakes and oceans could be safe resting areas, but we already know that deep in the oceans are volcanoes. We also know that the bottoms of the oceans are frequently covered in rare metals. The rocky desert areas are frequently connected to radioactive matter. You will see from military sightings the vessels are frequently seen at nuclear weapons sites. I do not think that they go to military sites to destroy or steal radioactive weapons. I think they go there to see if our human race has finally reached a point where they no longer concentrate on war. Remember, to go home you must have a pure heart. We came into this world helpless and pure. We should understand that we must leave this world helpless and pure.

"So, these were the sites where I had to begin my research. I was looking for a metal that we know nothing about or a metal that can be changed from something we know to something different. Just so you know I had met your next-door neighbor David and his wife Lynn and their lovely little daughter Nora. Ask him what we talked about. Once again, Jimmy, I was not hiding anything from you. As you will see I was hiding everything from everybody so that no one could have any idea as to what I was looking for.

"The metal that I was searching for was one that could change from solid to liquid if certain conditions were applied to it. Obviously, we know liquid metals and we know some metals that can change from solid to liquid at various temperatures. It was those that I began scientifically studying. They contained what I wish to find a metal with the possibility of possessing. The metal I was searching for was not something that was commonly used on the planet Earth. However, the basic form of it was here. We thought the changes could be made inside a volcano and we can create those forces. Therefore, we could change it to the metal that we need.

"We found it and we were able to change it and exactly how to do it is all in this chip. The key to the metal is how sharp can we make an extension so that it penetrates our universe in order to move into the 'In Between.' Have you ever seen a thousand time enlargement of a metal pin? You can see that the sharpest metal is still dull. However, if you look at a thousand time enlargement of the stinger on a bee it is unbelievably sharp. The pin and the stinger were made differently. We had to make the pin as the stinger was made. The bee stinger's formation is controlled by electromagnetic forces. We finally were able to bring the metal pin to a sharpness that may be only atoms across. It was all through magnetic forces. Once one atom of your pin crosses the barrier into the 'In Between' the rest quickly follows."

David reached over and paused the computer and said, "I suspect that I already know which metal has most of these properties. It kept coming to mind when Mark and I intensely discussed metals."

They hit the Play button on the computer, and Mark continued, "Once you are able to enter into the space between the two universes you are in a situation where neither universe wishes you to be there. It is a vacuum. There is no friction. That 'In Between' space has the exact opposite effect of friction. Friction, as you know, would slow down anything including light. Now you have a situation where the exact opposite occurs. Simply try to imagine the speed that you can attain in that space. There is no gravity. This is how the vessels travel. So many scientists say that if there was a vessel, it would take us hundreds of years to reach the nearest star. That certainly is true in our universe, but it is not true if you are in the space between the two universes. In that space neither our universe nor the dark universe want you to be there so instead of holding you, they push you.

"Later, I will explain to you the almost certain point that they all are trying to reach. Notice I used 'they.' It is not beings from one planet or even one galaxy. It is many and they are all going to the same place. So, should we? Isn't it funny that Paul and I had a long discussion with someone about this exact situation about eleven years ago. We were not talking about space travel. We were talking about the travel of our souls. The person who we were talking with was your grandmother, Tillie. She told us God was calling us home and we must be ready to go as soon as possible. She insisted home is heaven and she kept emphasizing one important statement that Jesus made. That statement was in the Beatitudes: The pure of heart will see God. Do you understand what that means? It is extremely important that you do understand it. Remember, no being or element or plasma can go home unless it is 'pure of heart.'

"The Dark Universe cannot truly enter our universe of origin. There is an 'In Between' barrier. However, what it can do is divide us. It could be tucked between our layers. If it is in our layers then we cannot go home. This is the battle that we fight. We have heard about the battle to become 'pure of heart,' There are combatants who have fought it and are fighting it today and why we have fought that battle over and over again through recorded history. Humans are not very attentive beings. The other species see this and that is the reason for virtually no contact. In order to go back to from where we came, we MUST be that entity. There can be no darkness. When you come to the point where you could re-enter your real universe, your home, you cannot bring any Dark Matter/Energy along for the ride."

They turned off the computer and sat in silence. Each one trying to understand what Mark had just shared. After a few minutes they looked at each other.

Jimmy then said, "The morning I left home to head back to college when I saw the vessel, my mom, Tillie, came up to the window of my car and said to me that I should remember that Jesus said take the narrow gate. Is there a connection?"

Melinda then said, "Let's shut it down for tonight."

They all agreed and that is exactly what they did.

<h1 style="text-align:center">CHAPTER 18</h1>

On the next morning, they were all up early. They gathered out on the porch to have coffee. Dave and Jimmy had gotten back on the chip to look at a footnote. What they were looking for was a list of people who Mark recommended that they talk to privately. They were people from Father Consolo, S.J. who was an astronomer and director of the Vatican Observatory. He recommended a famous metal laboratory. There was an attorney in Pittsburgh, Pennsylvania, a computer firm in Los Angeles, and a person in the press from Rochester, New York. The footnote said nothing more than that he strongly recommends that they speak to these people.

As they sat on the porch, David and Jimmy were sharing the names with their wives asking them if they knew any of these people? Both wives knew of Father Consolo. They were not sure of the rest on the list.

Lynn said, "It's best that we don't see these people as a group except for the attorney. Each of us can take a few of the names and arrange to see them on our own. We must not do anything at this time to let the government know that we have the chip."

They all agreed.

Jimmy said that there is a conference in Tucson, Arizona coming up in a couple of weeks. He then explained that Father Consolo does much of his research at the observatories at Kitt Peak National Observatory and that was located about fifty miles southwest of Tucson. He explained that if he and Melinda went to that conference one or both of them could slip away to meet with Father Consolo. Melinda interrupted and suggested that Lynn and she should go out to Los Angeles to speak to the computer people. So, Jimmy then said that was fine and he would try to arrange the trip to Tucson if the priest would be at Kitt Peak.

Dave said that he knew people at the metals laboratory where Mark said the one scientist with whom they should talk was connected. He would be able to check and see if the person that Mark spoke about still worked at that lab. If that person is still employed, then he would arrange a meeting through his lab.

They all agreed that some of them would talk to the newspaper person in Rochester face-to-face. Melinda said, "I know that Mark would not have recommended these people for no reason. I assume that he has already met with them quite a few times. We have to be very careful until we know why their names are on the chip."

David then pointed out, "Remember, only the second chip is to be released to the public."

Melinda thought there was enough time still off on her job at the NSA so that she could accompany Lynn out to Los Angeles. She was going to try to arrange an appointment with the attorney from Pittsburgh, if possible, before they leave.

Everyone was in agreement and they just went on with their day at the beach. Tonight, they would visit the chip again. The opportunities ahead must stay hidden. The protection that they are having on this trip will run out at some point. However, as Melinda explained they are always suspicious. It is part of the job to be suspicious, constantly.

That Saturday the weather was once again beautiful with blue skies and 80°F temperature. It was not too humid. The little girls had a wonderful day down at the beach. Once again, the day repeated itself. Down to the beach, then they went up for lunch, then down to the beach again. Wherever the kids went the parents went as well.

Melinda kept reminding them that she was quite certain that the attempt to observe them by the government was ongoing, but they have a tremendous advantage having this particular beach site. The government would even have difficulty getting close enough to use sound enhancement devices. Visual contact would be easy but sound capture would be hard. People do not realize that the crashing waves at any beach interferes with sound and you end up speaking much louder than you normally would speak. This group, however kept the intensity of their voices the same as if they were at the house. As it has always been in the specialty of spying, it is based on give-and-take. The government does not want you to know that they are observing you, but they must attempt to observe you. It is always mostly give-and-take. They spent the day just as anyone else would at the beach.

Later that night they were back on the computer. They replayed a little of the chip that they had heard the night before and then continued on to the new section.

On the screen Mark began by saying, "I guess you've wondered what type of power the craft that I've built will use. It's fusion power. I know that makes everybody become confused and concerned. Fusion power has not been used on Earth because it has been dangerous mainly due to the fact that they have tried fusion of hydrogen. Fusing hydrogen gives off too much uncontained power. Now, if you think of changing those elements of fusion to helium-3, then you have a very safe origin of power. There is no radioactivity. Of course, the problem was finding the helium-3. We know where it is, but it is difficult to get to because the closest places are the moon, asteroids, and Mars.

"I hope that you have figured it out that all of the recently planned missions to the moon were really not to do research per se. They are planning to mine for helium-3 and change our power source on Earth to fusion power. Our own safe and small suns. It was kept secret because of the political pressure and that pressure is money. The money to be obtained by the group that possesses the helium-3 is a fortune beyond anyone's imagination. Wouldn't you have loved to buy $1 million worth of Apple stock the first day it went public? This will be far beyond that profit.

"There is a company in Britain that can construct fusion power plant equipment. They know where this world is heading and they want to be ready for that moment when the world change over to fusion power occurs. So, I received the equipment and the only problem that I had to do solve was to find helium-3. That, however, is a bit difficult on this planet. You already know that helium-3 covers the moon and Mars and asteroids and other rocky planets that have no magnetic protection from the interior of the planet. Of course, the solar wind does get through to Earth. The solar wind is the deliverer of helium-3, but that magnetic glove of Earth is what blocks the helium-3. So, I had to find a place on Earth where that magnetic protection is at its minimum. To find the highest altitude in that area. Some helium-3 had to have made it in through the Earth's shield at that point. That is where I found it.

"Once you have some you have the power to leave this planet. Once you leave this planet it is easy to obtain more. The site on Earth is also the site where reports of these vessels have been made. The three areas that we searched were in Antarctica, the mountains of Chile, and Argentina and certain areas on the bottom of the Southern Ocean. We found it or at least we found enough of it to use it as the fuel for our fusion reactors. A small fusion plant is more than enough to produce all power that we will ever need. As you would expect, we built two small plants for the vessel. That is for safety and backup.

"Our goal is to travel in the In Between space for quite a distance and then come back... hopefully. That is how the beings from the other planets began as well. The fear of what can happen in the future is extremely high. Each felt that they had to save their race but each are finding out that we are all from the same origin. We are all doing it for the same reason and that is to preserve the energy who we are from the first day when we burst into this universe. We all need to go home.

"Hopefully, we will return and explain what we have found and what we have unraveled and where all of these other beings are going. It is to the same place. Our world, Earth, will want to do the same. There will be people opposed to the idea and people who desire go on this trip, but as time goes on the number who want to stay here will decrease to only a few. That means that it is the job of our planet to construct the vessels to make the trip.

"This planet will eventually face extinction of life. It may also face total destruction. It will not come from 'Global Warming.' It will be gamma rays or other radiation beams from exploding stars, black holes, magnetars from all parts of the universe. This is what is happening every second in the universe. It happened to whatever form that our energy was connected to before Earth even formed. In the beginning the Dark universe surrounded us. It surrounded the plasma that was us. It had no idea what we were, what we could do, what we would do. It is identical that we know nothing of it. The Dark Matter gathered us just as you saw the liquids inside that bottle I showed you. Shake the bottle and watch. We were gathered into clumps and we, not the Dark Matter, went on to form stars. Then the Dark Energy began to diffuse us. It tried to come between us.

"Now that allows me to explain why I am recommending that you all spread this information. One nation, one country, one political party is not the answer to achieving what is needed. The greatest sin of all human beings is control. If control is allowed into the picture, the picture falls apart. This has been conveyed to me. So, before our government understands the true nature of this project, we need to have the information spread around the globe."

They turned off the computer. They knew that the other chip contained all the technical information of building the vessels that will be able to do what needs to be done. At some point everyone needs to make this trip. We must, at some point, enter the 'In Between.' We must. In that space we will be protected. Our matter and energy are safe. Then we can head home.

There are also sites on the chip where Mark explains life inside of the vessel. He explained the functioning of the different sites. Eventually, they looked at each other and nodded. They knew what they must do.

CHAPTER 19

That evening they took the girls down to the beach to enjoy the end of the weekend break. Later, when they had gone back to the house and the girls were asleep in their bedroom, they brought out the small laptop computer. They put it down on the coffee table in front of them. They turned on the TV and had the volume on low. Melinda put the chip into the laptop and turned on the program.

Mark continues, "Needless to say, I found a metal alloy that would work for what I wanted. We then could do what they are doing. We could travel to any site we choose and if there is ever a time to listen to those travelers, it is now. For thousands of years they have been defining exactly where we should all be heading. If human beings were truly moral, I think that these travelers would have shared the reason as to where and why they are going. As you go back through many of the UFO sightings, you will find out that so many of them were near nuclear weapon storage facilities. We all thought for a while that they were interested in obtaining something nuclear, but that was not the case. They simply were concerned as to whether we would use these devastating weapons on all species on Earth. The human race could not come along on this trip if nuclear war was something they felt they needed.

"So, we did all of this research on our own. When I say 'our' I mean our group. The group is larger than you may realize. We came to understand how to make the travelers come to us. We were able to converse with them briefly. That is, they at least told us where they were going. They did not tell us how to do it because they were still afraid of the flaws of human beings. To accomplish building a vessel that can do what their vessels do, I needed, first of all, a metal alloy. I needed something that moved from hard metal to liquid controlled by temperature and magnetism. I found it. It was a cesium-glass alloy. There is a whole section on the other chip as to how to make it and specifically how to use it because the crucial use of this metal is when you want to gently puncture our universe as a liquid and slide into the space between our side and the side of the dark matter and energy."

Mark continues, "If you were traveling in the space In Between here on Earth and a person on Earth was so close to you she could see your vessel. What is seen is not as visually clear as it would be if neither she nor the vessel were in the In Between space. However, she could still see it. Remember what I told you about dark matter and dark energy. It is not dark. It is clear just like water, but it is different. Just like with water if you go under the surface you can see things close to you rather clearly but the farther away they move from you they begin to distort and eventually disappear. We cannot nor should we ever try to penetrate into that dark universe. It is not us. In fact, human beings on this planet and possibly other living beings on this planet in the past and beings from every planet whether living or inanimate throughout the universe have been told the same thing. We have been told to be ready to come home. These vessels that we now know are temporarily stopping on the planet Earth. Maybe refueling. Maybe taking in water, oxygen, or anything that they need.

"We are fairly sure that they know where home is because they all seem to be heading in the same direction. Throughout the history of humankind as far back as recorded history there have been codes and lists of instructions and consciences and Beatitudes all saying the same thing. It did not matter what the religion of any type would be because the message was always the same: 'Blessed be the pure of heart for they shall see God.' We were specifically told this incredibly important order. The sad thing is that no matter what religion, the flaws of human beings break those instructions. If you are wondering what the flaw actually is, I suspect that you already know. It is dark matter and dark energy. It does not become part of us, but it infiltrates between our parts. If we eliminated the dark matter and dark energy in us and around us we will have achieved 'Pure of Heart.'"

Mark continues, "So, there is our job. There is our home. This may be how we get to our real home. I know that millions of scientists will disagree about the actual occurrence of the Big Bang, but believe me, it was a collision and a rift and for an extremely short period of time plasma from our home, from our universe poured into this universe. It is a universe that belongs to the dark energy and the dark matter."

Mark then said, "We have been told that we will be saved and I believe that but there is a problem occurring. The dark energy is spreading us apart. As the distance between us gets farther Einstein's 'riddle' may collapse. Think of it like a piece of taffy and as you pull both ends of any piece of matter from our universe apart the part between is not empty space. The piece of our universe gets thinner and thinner and perhaps in the long run it may break. That is what Dark Energy believes. However, according to the riddle, it does not. That is why this journey was started. As of today, as long as the thin connection between us is still present, then the 'In Between' is still present. If the 'In Between' is present, then we have an opportunity to get back to that area of the universe where the collision occurred.

"I suspect you already know that an area far out in the universe has been visualized and described as a bruise. That is where everyone is heading. Perhaps God gave us the opportunity to understand this for a specific reason. Perhaps he wants us to travel. If we never did anything that would make our hearts impure perhaps that is when we should go. This is the reason that I included several people that you should speak with about their contribution to this plan. They are trustworthy, but I understand that you need to make that decision on your own."

"Remember, the proposed current maps of the universe show the spreading that is occurring and you actually SEE the pulled taffy description. You see the connections that are already present but in jeopardy. The jeopardy is what we race against. Now, we can accomplish the travel. We need to do the travel."

Jimmy reached over and put the program on pause. Everyone sat staring at Mark's face on the screen of the computer and not a single word was spoken. They just stared because their minds were functioning at an incredible pace.

David then quietly said, "Let's spend some time thinking about what Mark just said."

They turned off the computer.

Lynn then advised, "We're going to need copies of both chips. How that copy is obtained is something we will have to discuss."

Everyone agreed.

CHAPTER 20

On Sunday morning the adults got up at about seven o'clock and shared the work of personal packing and group packing. They cleaned the house efficiently. At nine o'clock they were getting into their cars and heading back toward Washington, DC. Not a single person spoke about the real reason for the weekend at the beach nor while they were driving home. That approach shows their trust in the United States Government intelligence programs. Melinda and Jim already work for the United States Government. Melinda works for one of the most complicated intelligence departments. They had quietly discussed that it is most likely that at least four United States intelligence organizations are directed at them. Melinda had not been contacted by her employer... yet.

It was a sunny day and the traffic was not that bad, although it did tighten up around the Bay Bridge. As always all caravans leaving anywhere together by automobile still dissipate after the first five to ten miles. So, each never sought each other's car after that point and yet they arrived in their neighborhood in Washington, DC about the same time. Jimmy thought, *truly amazing. I never see them for 150 miles. We must have been an extremely short distance between each other for the entire trip. Truly amazing.*

They unpack at home and notice that there is a message for Jimmy on the answering machine. It was from Agent Haas at the FBI asking if he would come down on Monday at one o'clock for a quick meeting. Agent Haas left a number to call simply to verify that he will be there. Jimmy did that.

As evening came Melinda and Jimmy were sitting on some comfortable lounges in their backyard and grilling some corn and hotdogs for supper. This is their daughter's favorite combination.

At one point Melinda asked Jimmy, "You're still going to be going to that astrophysics conference at the Marriott in Tucson Arizona next week. Right?"

Jimmy said, "Yes. They want me to do one small talk at the conference, but I'll be going mostly to listen. Some of the new concepts on all aspects of astrophysics are enlightening."

Melinda then says, "I don't have to get back to work for about two weeks and Lynn and I were talking about heading out to the West Coast for a few days."

Jimmy asks, "To do?"

She answered, "For me to go to LA. Nothing special except to be with Lynn."

She wrote on a napkin: *See the computer specialist that Mark mentioned.* "We have all those insurance airplane miles from the trip last year when we all were going out to Los Angeles, but had to cancel it when something came up at work. It is sure perfect to not have any explanation to the airline industry why you had to cancel a trip if you work for the NSA."

Melinda continues, "Lynn is the one who suggested that we go to that destination. She wants to meet with another computer genius in Los Angeles for some project that she's currently working. I just thought it would be a good idea since you'll be heading to Tucson and we can be away at the same time. We can get our baby sitter to watch the kids."

Jimmy says, "Sounds great to me. I wish life were kind enough to let us do everything together, but we had this past weekend and with God's help there will be more in the future."

They then went to bed early and held each other tightly all night long. Each wanted to keep talking, but each knew that they needed more to not talk about. The next morning they were both up by six o'clock. In so many locations around the world you can get up and get ready and get to work in an hour. Not Washington, DC. It is more likely three hours. Most people who come to Washington, DC to work for the first time in the US Capitol and are driving to work for the first day begin to wonder *"Did all of these people just receive their driver's license yesterday?"* They say that Boston is the most dangerous place to drive because they have the most dangerous drivers. Washington, DC is the most incompetent place.

Jimmy gets down to work at his office by around nine o'clock. He talks to several people about what a great time he had over the weekend at the beach. He asked his secretary to be sure to get his ticket verified from Dulles to Tucson Arizona.

At around 11:30, he decides that rather than drive over to Agent Haas's office, he would call an Uber. He was a minute or two late and went in and went through the same introduction at the front desk as he did the last time he was there. He is shown down the corridor to the same conference room that he had met with Agent Haas for the last meeting.

Haas comes in about one minute after Jimmy arrived. He smiles and shakes his hand and immediately asks, "You haven't heard from Dr. O'Donnell, have you?"

Jimmy says, "I told you I would let you know." Then he asks, "Have you found Mark yet?"

Haas ignores Jimmy's question and then mentions, "I tried to reach you on Saturday, but you weren't home. I tried again on Sunday."

Jimmy then slowly says, "You know exactly where I was. That's your job."

Haas then smiles but says nothing. He sat silently for a minute and then slowly begins to stand up and tells Jimmy, "I told you this would be a quick meeting."

Jimmy answers, "Of course, I knew it would be a quick meeting because there is nothing for us to discuss."

They shake hands and Agent Haas escorts Jimmy out to his secretary and then says, "I'll be in touch."

CHAPTER 21

Jimmy is driving a rental car from the Tucson Airport to the Marriott Hotel located in a valley west of the city. The road from the airport is initially quite straight, but once you begin to wind your way into the canyon where the hotel is located, you realize the difference between man deciding the road and the geography deciding the road. He pulled into the check-in semicircle. He told the valet that he will be personally parking his car and he was just going to check in. He did unload his bag and gave it to the bellhop with a tip and asked him to take it up to his room.

He then drove down the winding road between the Marriott Hotel in the surrounding golf course until he reached the entrance to the parking garage. In Tucson, Arizona it is nice to be able to park under a roof. Hot is a good description of the weather. Jimmy parked his car as close as possible to the elevator that takes you to the hotel. He grabbed his carry-on case. He locked the car and headed in to the hotel. It was a comfortable walk up to his room.

It is the day before the conference begins, so he puts on his bathing suit, grabs his sandals, his laptop, and heads down to the closest pool. He sees some professors from Berkeley who are old friends. They see him heading over toward them and, with smiling faces, they shake his hand and tell Jimmy it is great to see him again. They all sit down and begin discussing one of their favorite topics—college sports. Because of the heat, he spends a few hours in and out of the pool. Jimmy asks his old friends what they're doing for dinner? They said they would be eating at the hotel and that he should join them.

Jimmy says, "That sounds great I'll see you at…?"

They told him they had a table reserved for seven o'clock and Jimmy said that he would see them then.

When Jimmy got to his guestroom he called his wife but there was no answer. He knew that she was flying with Lynn to Los Angeles and then he realized they would still be in flight. He thought he would just try to call her later this day or tomorrow morning. He went out onto the little porch off of his guestroom with a glass of ice water. He put on his sunglasses and stared out at the beautiful view sweeping down the valley toward Tucson. One thing that you can always be sure you will find in Tucson is sunshine. As evening comes and the sun begins to set in the west the ground changes color. Whites and tans become pinks and oranges allowing the true beauty of a desert to encapsulate you. Tucson as a city is basically flat, but as you move into the suburbs to the west and to the east, the ground begins to curve upward toward Mount Lemmon in the East and toward Tucson Mountain Park in the West. The Marriott Hotel sits in one of the valleys leading toward Tucson Mountain Park.

He has a great dinner with his friends later that evening. He registers for the course before joining them for dinner. He spoke to the chairman of the course for a few minutes and found out that he will not be speaking until early Saturday morning. Since this day was Thursday that would give him a portion of Friday to accomplish what this trip to Tucson is actually about.

For the remainder of the day he went to every lecture and later had dinner with his same friends at the hotel. He got up very early the next morning. He got in his car and he headed west. He drove his car curving up through the Tucson Mountain Park. On the other side he was suddenly looking at a vast, completely dry ocean. At one point in Earth's past it would have been a body of water, but today it is desert. Cactus of so many types spread through the completely flat land.

He headed west and later turned north toward the Coyote Mountain Wilderness area. He drove first through the valley to the east of Coyote Mountain Wilderness. On the northern side he got on the two-lane highway and headed west toward Kitt Peak National Observatory. It took about an hour from Tucson to Kitt Peak. He drove up the mountain through turns and dips and ended in a parking area next to the telescopes at Kitt. He chose a place to park and then got out of his car and began walking toward the main observatory. Many people may think that Kitt Peak is nothing more than a few observatories on the top of the mountain but that's not the case. There are numerous buildings along with several observatories spread out across the top of the peak.

You rarely see people outside of the buildings and that is not because it's too hot. It is not that hot on the top of Kitt Peak. The reason you do not see them is because they are working inside. Each doing hundreds of specific projects.

Jimmy was not up on Kitts Peak to use the Observatory. He was there to talk to an astronomer. His name was Father Guy Consolo. Father Consolo was the head of the Vatican Observatory. However, he spends part of the year in Rome at the Vatican Observatory and the rest of his working time on Kitts Peak.

Jimmy had been to Kitts Peak in the past but Father Consolo was never there when Jimmy was there. At least, to his knowledge. So, he had never met Father or Dr. Consolo.

He followed a path that led into the back door of one of the observatories. He knew that door was not locked, so he quietly let himself in. At first there seemed to be no one present inside the observatory. We humans, however, have an odd ability to sense the presence of another living being in our presence. He quietly walked closer to the base of the telescope and that is when he saw Father Consolo. What he saw was a man with salt-and-pepper hair and salt-and-pepper beard who was bent over an instrument connected to the telescope.

Jimmy then said, "I'm not sure how I'm supposed to address you? Would it be Doctor or Father?"

Father Consolo did not raise his head. He just kept working at what he was doing. There was a pause of a few seconds and then, still not looking at Jimmy, Father Consolo quietly says, "It all depends on why you're here?"

Scientists think differently than non-scientists. If you could read their minds you probably would laugh. They approach everything as a puzzle. This is not upsetting to them. It is normal to them.

Jimmy said, "I'm here to talk to you about Dr. Mark O'Donnell."

Father Consolo said nothing for a few seconds and then said, "In that case, I suspect Father would be the better choice."

Jimmy waits a second and then says, "Well, Father Consolo, my name is Jimmy Loftus. Mark and I went to MIT together and—"

Father Consolo quietly interrupts and says, "I know who you are, Jimmy."

"I presume that you know of me from Mark?" Jimmy asks.

Father Consolo seems a bit cautious in what he says and does not answer that question but he then asks, "How is Mark?"

Jimmy states, "I suspect you already know that I would not have any idea how he is at this particular moment."

Father Consolo is looking down at the area of the telescope he was working on and begins rubbing it with what appeared to be an extremely soft cloth. After a few moments, without looking up, he asks, "Has he left?"

He did not expect that question. He answers, "Yes, I believe he has and I suspect you know why I am here."

Father Consolo looks up from his tinkering and directly into Jimmy's eyes and says, "Yes, I suspect I do."

Father Consolo continues and says to Jimmy, "With a name like Loftus I suspect that you were raised in the Catholic religion. I am correct—right?"

Jimmy answers, "I have been. I am. And I will be."

Father Consolo put down the cloth and continues to look Jimmy directly into his eyes. He has a face that makes you want to smile the moment you see it. Extremely rare in human beings is this countenance. Salt and pepper surrounding incredibly blue eyes and a captivating smile. That smile is not unique to priests. They are the persons who, like all people, interact with other people in all situations, but if the situation is a painful one, most people to some extent run away. Everyone knows that those situations need to be brought to be still. The priest has a unique gift of bringing stillness.

Father Consolo continues, "Many years ago Mark told me what you saw. Did what you see affect your faith?"

Jimmy then smiled and answered, "I suspect it should have, but it did not. Oddly enough it made my faith stronger and I never could understand why, but it did."

Father Consolo almost whispers, "When we as humans confront something that is far beyond anything we knew, then we, if we have a strong faith, rely on God to help us deal with what we had just experienced." Father Consolo asked, "What about now? I'm going to presume that since you're here to talk to me, Mark has already told you what he found. You're Catholic. You worship the Trinity. Of the Three the one who may come into question would be Jesus. You may see that intellectually, but you know the truth. Am I correct?"

Jimmy answers, "I take my religion quite seriously. I suspect that some people would have trouble understanding what Jesus was handing to us when they find out there are aliens in the universe."

He continues, "My faith in Jesus became stronger. Those whose faith would weaken are people who think that they themselves are God. I was once in the restaurant of a hotel in Williamsburg, Virginia visiting a family member who was in a hospital nearby. I was sitting at a table all alone when two men and two teenage boys came up to my table and asked if it is okay if they sat down with me because all the other tables are taken. I said, 'Sure. Please sit down.'

"We did courteous chitchatting for a little while and then one of the fathers told me that they were there on a religious retreat with their sons. I said that was nice. He then went on to ask me what are my thoughts about how God allows certain things to occur. Things that are atrocious. I said to him, quietly, that there is something that they ought to know and that is that if you took every single grain of sand from every beach in the world and from the bottom of every ocean in the world and from every desert in the world and made a huge pile of sand, that is God. What we know, as humans, is basically one grain of sand. I then said that priests and ministers and rabbis probably have two grains of sand.

"So, you see that the presence of aliens from outer space would not be enough to make me think and believe anything different than I have ever believed before."

Jimmy then said, "When I finally met up with Mark after quite a few years we did not specifically talk about this topic. However, he left a chip and on that chip he does address this topic. It was on the chip that he directed me to you and several other people. We made copies of the chips and I have yours today. On that chip is everything. I mean everything. Every aspect of his research. Everything that he found. How he was able to construct a vessel that will function exactly like the vessel I saw that October morning in Western Massachusetts ten-plus years ago. Every detail of every aspect of his research is right there."

Father Consolo says nothing.

Jimmy continues, "Did he ask you to go along with him when he left?"

Father Consolo answers, "Yes, he did. However, as you see, I am here. I am not here because I was afraid. I am an astronomer and you would have to be insane to turn down an offer of this magnitude. However, I am also a priest and that part of my life far outweighs the study of the stars. I am here for you. I am here for your family. I am here for your friends. I am here for your enemies. I am here for all humans just as I was asked to do by Jesus."

Jimmy then says, "If the entire world began to build these vessels I suspect that you, Father, would only be on the very last one. Am I correct?"

Father Consolo smiles and says, "Yes, you are correct.

"The purpose behind all of this is to try to save our universe. It is unexpectedly generating gamma rays that destroy other areas of the universe. The dark energy is spreading our universe to a point where there will be a single particle billions of miles from another particle. It is heading to the end. I assume that Mark has explained that what we describe as our universe is in actuality the dark universe. It is a different universe that we accidentally broached. For an extremely short period of time our original energy poured into the dark universe and then it was stopped. The defect closed. We were trapped."

Father Consolo then quietly said, "We want to go home. There were times when humans thought the dark universe was our universe. Today we and soon everyone will want to go home. Go home to our true universe."

They then went on talking about the secrecy of the chip. Jimmy explained that there were several people all around the world who would be receiving this chip. He said at this time everyone must be quiet. Father Consolo did not say anything, but Jimmy had no question whatsoever that he completely understood what he was being told.

As Father Consolo and Jimmy walked out to his car, they stopped and then they shook hands and promised to meet again. Jimmy then drove the long road back to his conference in Tucson.

Chapter 22

Lynn and Melinda's flight from Dulles Airport to Los Angeles went without problems. After landing they collected their luggage and hired a taxi. They had no intention of driving in Los Angeles for the same reason people do not like to drive in Washington, DC. Lynn knows Los Angeles. Her firm is "Recreate." It is a company that rather than tearing down a struggling business, they would study every aspect of the business with regard to time being in business, employees, purpose, economics, and expectations of the future. Not the future of the business, rather the future of the United States and other countries in the world.

They took the cab to their hotel just north of downtown Los Angeles. They went to their rooms and quickly freshened up from the flight. They called ahead to the company, Computer Creation, to confirm their appointment. A friendly secretary answered the phone and assured them of their appointment. They went down to the lobby and hailed another taxi and gave the driver the address of Computer Creation.

They arrived at the office building and took the elevator up to the fifth floor and entered the artfully decorated doors leading to the corporation. The entrance was decorated in a sky theme. There were only two people in the waiting room. The secretary was behind the front desk. One of the persons sitting in the waiting room was a young man with curly brown hair working on a laptop. He seemed intensely focused on whatever he was doing. The other person in the waiting room was a young woman. She seemed somewhat distracted. She kept glancing out the window. Lynn and Melinda went up to the front desk and introduced themselves and reminded the secretary that they had an appointment with Brennan Ford. He was one of the owners of the corporation. Oddly, the secretary looked at them directly and then let her eyes slowly move to the right where she was looking at the young man in the waiting room. Her gaze came immediately back to them and she did the same thing again. A very slow smile came to her face and her head nodded. In other words, she was telling Melinda and Lynn that their appointment was with the young man sitting in the waiting room. Both of them slowly turned and looked at him and then the secretary said, "Dr. Ford, your appointment has arrived."

Dr. Ford's gaze quickly elevated from his laptop to their eyes and then a smile broke out on his face. He quickly jumped up and came over to them and said, "Hi. My name is Brennan. Let's go down to my office."

He opened the door to the inner offices for them and then he quicky got in front of them so that they could follow him. They kept glancing at each other. They obviously both had the same question—*Why was he in the waiting room?* They went through another door leading to the inner office and as they walked down the corridor, both women thought that since he was an owner of the corporation, his office would be the bigger room. They passed several extremely large offices including a beautiful corner office, but they kept walking. Eventually they came down to a moderately sized office and he opened the door and they walked in and he followed them. In the office there was a desk, chair, a sofa, and nothing else.

He said to them, "Please have a seat." He then went behind his desk and sat down. He looked at them again and then said, "And the purpose for your visit is?"

Melinda answered and said, "This visit has to do with Dr. Mark O'Donnell."

Dr. Ford's eyes opened wider and he stood up from his desk and came over to the sofa and said, "Could you move over?"

Computer experts are different around the country. In Los Angeles they do not concentrate on one thing. In fact, they do not really concentrate on any thing. They concentrate on the space in a room rather than the room. Their minds are like controlled explosions. Movies are made or started in Los Angeles. If you start with a production being "A," it will quite likely end up being "Z." In New York if it starts out being "A," it will most likely end up being "A" or being close to it. They are most interested in the facts for computer software. In Los Angeles, there are no facts. It is "what you want."

They did and he sat down on the sofa.

He began, "Just so you know, this office cannot be tapped. I guarantee you." He continued. "Did Dr. Mark send you?"

Lynn answered, "In a way." She then went on to explain the story.

Brennan then asked, "Has Dr. Mark left this planet?"

Both women simultaneously answered, "We think so."

Brennan then smiled and said, "Oh yeah." He then continued, asking, "Did he tell you what I did?"

Melinda said, "We assumed that you did his computer work."

Brennan said, "Not computer work. Computer building. Computer building for a vessel that can virtually go anywhere. I created the real HAL. You know. HAL like in the movie *2001*. Or I should say my wife and I created the real HAL and it was spectacular. When we were finished we constructed a backup and that was an absolute duplicate of the original. It took five years, but everything was there. If I wanted to go to sleep for twenty years, HAL would take over. Every aspect of function of that vessel was included. There was 3D copy and construction, computerized medicine, navigation, power, vessel thrust, food creation, oxygen recreation, constant evaluation of every function of the vessel and everyone on the vessel."

He just went on and on.

Suddenly the door to his office opened and a beautiful Asian woman came charging into the room. She had a smile on her face. It was his wife, Fawn.

She immediately said to Brennan, "I know we have this arrangement that we are not to ever know what the other person is doing, but when it came down to this work I asked our secretaries to make an exception and contact me immediately when someone from Dr. Mark's outstanding project shows up at the office."

Brennan then said, "I was going to have our secretary call you anyway."

Fawn replied, "Really?" She then said to Brennan, "Scoot over." Brennan moved over on the couch letting Fawn sit closer to Melinda and Lynn.

Brennan then continued. "He warned me that once we got the word out there would be interference from our government and possibly from other governments as well. You know that I must not share any aspect of what we and his crew are doing with any single group, right?"

Melinda and Lynn then went on to tell him about the current attempts by the United States government to obtain information. They explained that to their knowledge nothing has gotten out.

Melinda then said, "There will come a time when all involved in this connection will come under investigation. You understand that, don't you?"

Brennan answered, "Of course, we understand that. I love intrigue. The purpose of what we are all doing is far too great to put into the hands of one country and definitely too great to put into the hands of one person in each country."

Lynn asked, "Obviously, your wife was involved in the meetings with Mark?"

Brennan quickly responds, "Oh yes. Fawn was here for each meeting with Mark and 'the smile.'"

Both women looked at each other quizzically and then Melinda said, "We assume that Fawn is your wife but who is 'the smile'?"

Brennan asked, "You haven't met Johnny Cosmar? He is the builder. He came with Mark the first time that Fawn and I met Mark and then he came by himself several times and he always has a smile on his face. Truly captivating. Have you ever met anybody like that? What I mean is have you ever met anybody whose mouth and eyes are smiling all the time? Constantly smiling no matter what the person is saying to you?"

He continues, "He is an extremely friendly guy. He is also the person you would want building your home. He is extremely specific. Over the ensuing months as Fawn, our staff, and myself began constructing the software and the computer, he was very specific as to where in the vessel they wanted the computer to be located. They wanted it to be central. Almost dead center in the vessel. If we suggested that it be even a few inches off left or right he would, with a smile on his face, say no. I remember one day when he was here and Fawn suggested that in any triangular structure sometimes placing the computer slightly forward or slightly backward from the position that he was asking for would be helpful."

Brennan then smiled and said, "He answered Fawn… smiling… and said 'Who said it was triangular?' Both Fawn and I looked at him and told him that we saw a rough draft of the vessel and it was triangular."

He then looked at us and said, "We are asking you to build the computer. Our job is to build the vessel and perhaps the vessel changes shape."

Brennan continued. "I'll tell you that comment certainly caused widening of my eyes. I think it was the first time that any of us thought that a structure can change its shape. Truly amazing. Much later we found out how they can do this 'shape change.'"

Fawn then looked at the two women and said, "Imagine that. From that point on we were looking at constructing something different from anything a human had ever thought they were capable of doing. Both Mark and Johnny assured us that they have information on certain points that we would not know anything about at that time. They asked us to secretly contact them anytime we come upon a problem and we did not have an answer. Otherwise, they were totally trusting us. Amazing, isn't it?"

The women then explained to Fawn and Brennan that they are here not only to meet them but to ask them to find the safest methods of communication over the computer or some other device that cannot be intercepted by the government.

Fawn and Brennan looked at each other, smiled and said, "No problem."

The women stood up and said, "Well, if Dr. Mark trusted you, then you certainly have our trust."

Fawn said, "Watch your computer mail and look for a spam advertisement on a home exercise program that has the name Excelsar. Download that and we will be able to get the information to you through a more direct but secret route. Without the first, the second will be worthless."

They got up and headed down the corridor and just before they entered the waiting room Brennan said with a huge smile on his face, "What a trip, right?"

Lynn answered, "You better believe it."

She then added, "How come you're not on that vessel now?"

Brennan looked her directly into her eyes and said, "Oh, there's a reason for that and you'll find out."

Chapter 23

Jimmy caught a red-eye flight from Tucson back to Washington, DC. It was just after midnight, but he was able to obtain an Uber from the airport to his home. He had called the babysitter who was watching his little girl and let her know what time to expect him. Lynn and David's daughter, Nora, was being watched by a different babysitter to help David when he was at work. They had talked about having one babysitter, but it was felt to be best at this time to make the families seem farther apart from each other.

He got to the house and thanked the babysitter excessively. She had her own car and headed on back to her apartment. His daughter was asleep and he ended up to their bedroom and did not even unpack from the trip. He peeked into his daughter's bedroom and saw that she was sound asleep. He simply got dressed for sleep and set the alarm for 6:00 A.M. He lay down on the mattress and almost instantly fell asleep. His dreams, however, that night were integrally woven into the entire trip that he just experienced.

He actually awakened before his alarm went off. He got up and went down to the kitchen and made some coffee. He knew Melinda would be arriving around eleven o'clock that morning. He took the coffee out onto the deck over the backyard of his house. He sat on one of the lounge chairs and sipped his coffee. If you asked him what at he was staring, his truthful answer would be "nothing." He would be telling the truth. Sometimes we simply look inward.

At seven o'clock his daughter got up, came down to the kitchen, and rushed out onto the deck to hug her daddy. She then went into a detailed explanation of every minute of everything she did over the entire weekend. Jimmy loved those stories. He called into work and told them he wouldn't be in until one o'clock in the afternoon. He had to wait until Melinda got back in from the West Coast and he simply wanted to spend time with his daughter. He knew that neither Melinda nor himself would be talking about their real trips. He would be talking about the conference and Melinda would be talking about interesting people she met in Los Angeles.

At around noon Melinda arrived. It was a scene of three people hugging and kissing. His daughter then went through the same explanation of her entire weekend. Kids are not that interested in what Mom or Dad did when they are away. They are only interested that they are back.

Jimmy whispered to Melinda, "There is an attorney whose name is John Murtaugh. He was a friend of Paul's. After they graduated from Harvard, Paul, of course, went into economics at the University of Pennsylvania, but John stayed at Harvard and went to law school. He lives and practices law in Pittsburgh, Pennsylvania. He dropped me a message saying that he would be in DC for a conference and that we should get together."

As Jimmy said this, Melinda saw his eyes become wider and his forehead wrinkle a bit. This was the silent method of telling her that Murtaugh was somehow connected to this entire situation.

"In any case," he continues, "I told him he can come over here for dinner or we can go out for dinner and we both agreed that it's your decision." He said this with a smile.

Melinda said, "Let's go out for dinner."

Jimmy agreed. "That would've been my choice as well."

Melinda then asked, "When is he getting in?"

Jimmy said, "Thursday morning."

Melinda smiles and says, "Perfect."

They then lowered their voices.

She whispers, "I know that I've heard of him. Have I?"

Jimmy answers, "Most people have never heard of him, but people who need to get into the deep intricacies of the law know exactly who he is. He wins whatever case he is involved in, you never hear his name in the press, and every single attorney knows exactly who he is. He does not make mistakes and he is feared by the opposition."

"Well, this will be an interesting dinner? Do you agree?" Melinda slowly whispers.

Jimmy answers, "That I guarantee you."

Jimmy goes upstairs and gets dressed for work. He heads off around 12:30 P.M. He drives to work and there is no congestion in the traffic. His mind is on his recent meeting with the priest/astronomer. Here was a situation in which he was discussing topics that would almost certainly be banned at MIT and any other modern-day astrophysics department. It is not that the population on the planet would not want to discuss these topics. It is the trap of science that wishes to believe that they can prove or disprove anything. They are such fools.

He begins thinking about his upcoming discussion with Murtaugh. He suspected that Murtaugh is more than aware of every single problem that has arisen, is currently arising, and will be arising in the future. The problem will never be with the material. The problem, as always, will only be with individual people. It is the greatest disease of mankind—Control Psychosis. It manages to kill far more human beings than any disease, any catastrophe, any war. It is one of the mysteries of the human race. How can someone with this addiction manipulate people into putting them in charge of countries?

He thinks, *I suspect we will hear Johnny's explanation of how we'll deal with this country-destroying problem.*

He arrives at work and is happily greeted by his secretary and other people at work. Each asking them about the conference. Some of the scientists asking whether he thought that they should attend the next conference covering those topics.

Of course, he said yes.

At three o'clock he receives a phone call from Agent Haas at the FBI.

Haas begins their conversation by saying, "You know you passed your screening." He then was silent.

Jimmy says, "I would presume I would pass it."

Haas is still quiet for a moment and then he asks, "How was your meeting out in Tucson?"

Jimmy answers, "It was fine."

Haas is quiet again. He then says, "I'm sure it was." He then continues. "Did you only go to the conference?"

Jimmy says, "Well, that is for you to find out. Maybe I went to a movie."

Haas is silent again and then says, "Well, I'll get back to you with some other questions at some point."

Jimmy answers, "Fine."

For the rest of the day he keeps thinking, *It will be interesting to meet with Murtaugh. I'll follow every action that he recommends. I'll follow them and I'll explain them to everybody involved.*

Chapter 24

On Thursday evening David and Lynn joined Jimmy and Melinda at the restaurant in Georgetown. The restaurant was Café Milano. They were there to meet Murtaugh. All week they discussed having the dinner at a different restaurant on purpose. The one they talked about was the Filomena Ristorante. They even made reservations at that restaurant, but they also made reservations secretively at the Café Milano. A half hour before dinner they canceled their reservations at the Filomena Ristorante.

The Café Milano would be the perfect site. It has fabulous cuisine, but it is also a Capitol Hill members and lobbyists meeting site because sound does not travel in that restaurant. What you say at your table does not seem to be heard very well at adjacent tables. There are not many restaurants that have this feeling of security. When people go to a restaurant that has this attribute and finish their meal they find themselves thinking how comforted they felt at that restaurant. They cannot put their finger on what it is that is producing that feeling. It is this safety and protection that they experienced. This restaurant gave them security, but they were not even aware of it.

Melinda touches Jimmy's hand and whispered to the others, "Look off to the right."

From near the entrance to the restaurant a tall man was approaching them. Melinda thought he had blond hair or gray hair or a mixture. He was about six foot one and had a handsome face and she was not sure, but he seemed to be smiling at them. He walked up to the table and she could see he actually was smiling at them. He looked down at everybody and rubbed his hands together and said, "I know you don't know me, but my—"

He was interrupted by another person who was moving toward their table and both Jimmy and Melinda knew him. It was Attorney John Murtaugh.

When he saw Jimmy, Murtaugh smiled and shook Jimmy's hand. He looked at David and Lynn, and Jimmy said, "Johnny, this is David and Lynn Cox. They are involved."

Murtaugh then introduced the new gentleman who had just approached their table, saying, "This gentleman is Ed Malm. He also is involved."

They both sat down. When the group reserved the table initially they were told to reserve two seats. Jimmy thought it would be for Murtaugh's wife. Obviously, it was not his wife and the subject was dropped.

Ed Malm begins by saying, "I know that you do not know me, but I do know about half of you." He gestured toward Jimmy and Melinda." As he said this he was smiling. His smile was engaging. The right side of his mouth turned up higher in a smile than the left side and then at other times the left side would turn up higher than the right. Melinda was fixated on this since she had never seen this before.

Ed continued, saying, "I met Mark through Johnny."

Murtaugh then said, "Ed is an extremely talented individual. What he will be doing for our group is something that no one ever thinks about. As time goes by listen carefully to what Ed tells you."

David asks Ed, "What is it exactly that you do for a living?"

Murtaugh and Ed looked at each other and smiled, and then Murtaugh said, "He is an expert in advertising. When I say an expert, I mean an *expert*."

The other four people glanced at each other. Murtaugh was correct. Ed quickly named just a few projects that are ongoing and directed by him. They would never have thought of this as something necessary for what they will soon be doing.

Murtaugh began by saying, "I'll get to the legal aspect of this shortly, but I need you to know what Ed will be doing. His job is to attract and educate all people. He will change their preference to accepting what we will be doing and he must start it with no one being aware that he is connected to our group."

Jimmy asked Ed, "What approach will you be attempting?"

Ed leaned forward and whispered, "Not attempting. Accomplishing. The projects are for everywhere and to everyone in every country."

Melinda said, "Isn't that rather extensive?"

Murtaugh then says, "Of course it is, but that is why we have Ed. I assume that you all are aware of the type of thinking called Lateral Thinking?"

They all nodded, but the women seemed to understand more than the men what Lateral Thinking actually is when practiced.

Murtaugh then said, "Let Ed explain it to you."

Ed began. "The classic description of the effectiveness of Lateral Thinking is the true story of an office building in New York City that was getting thousands of complaints about waiting for the elevator. The owners of the building hired engineers and increased the speed on the elevators, but the complaints continued. They then had some of the elevators go to certain floors and others go to other floors, but the complaints continued.

"Someone recommended that they get a consultation with a doctor who was the expert on Lateral Thinking. They did just that. The doctor came by and over the span of a week rode the elevators, watched the elevators, spoke to the people riding the elevators. Two weeks later he came back and presented his recommendation. What he recommended was that all the walls and the ceiling at the elevator at each floor be covered with mirrors. The owners of the building laughed and asked him how could that possibly fix the elevator problem? He simply said, 'Just do it.'

"They did just that and after the mirrors were installed virtually all of the complaints disappeared. That is Lateral Thinking. The whole idea is to captivate people's minds without them ever being aware that they have been captivated. NOT captive. Captivated." He continued. "We will not be tricking people into believing what we are doing is correct. We will be allowing their minds to understand that what we do is correct and they will know that they are right. It will also suggest that those opposing it are wrong."

Ed then said, "So, over time you will not be told exactly what I am doing but you will know that what I am doing is working."

Melinda, Jimmy, Lynn, and David all looked at each other and smiled then turned toward Ed and nodded their heads.

Murtaugh then began talking to them about the legal complications of releasing Mark's information around the world. He explained that certain countries and certain governments will accept it thankfully but others will take the exact opposite approach. He explained that he had been working on this probability for over five years.

He explained to them, "The only government that can approach you is our government and I am already five years ahead of anything they may attempt to do. So, no matter how scary the threat or action that they bring against you may seem, I want you to have faith. They will release stories to the press that will not be true. This is classic of our current government. They will pay professors to make claims that are untrue. I always want you to remember that legally we will always be ahead of them and where we want this to end up is in a State Supreme Court. They will think that some of their justices in the lower courts will decide against you, but I have already constructed the path and when you hear it you will think that I made a huge mistake. I did not make a huge mistake. It is almost as if we used Lateral Thinking to lure them down that path. As usual, our government is political and Ed has an ability to change politicians' thought processes. Politicians are not trustworthy in that they primarily care about themselves. First, simply to get elected then reelected. The people come in far second, but if we can control what the people think, then we control what the politician does."

He then continued. "Unfortunately, there are people connected to governments who are criminal. Medically they are known as individuals who suffer from an illness called Control Psychosis. These people are extremely dangerous. Some are elected and some are appointed. In all my years in law I have never truly understood how some of these people are elected into office. I just cannot understand why any human being would vote for them? But if you go through world history you see them—Hitler, Stalin, Mao, and on and on. They appear in country after country and through brutal force or through unexplained elections manage to get control. That is what we'll be fighting against. We will end up in the Supreme Court."

CHAPTER 25

At the end of their meal Lynn and Dave, Melinda and Jimmy, and Murtaugh and Ed left separately. They headed back to their homes or hotels. Both couples wanted to talk about the dinner and what they learned, but after hearing what Murtaugh warned them about, they talked about other things. Lynn and David talked about Nora in school and family members who they felt they should visit soon. Melinda and Jimmy for the same reason talked about similar topics. Both couples knew the enormity of what they had learned during their trip to the beach. They knew what could be said aloud and what must be kept secret.

Before dinner Jimmy and David had discussed running a trip up to the area in New York where Mark's laboratory was located. They had no intention of hiding this trip from the overlooking government. The purpose of their trip, however, was not to visit the lab site. Mark had suggested rather strongly that they speak with a man from Rochester, New York. His name is Michael Letsnew and he is a journalist. Both Jimmy and David had worries about speaking to a journalist. One never really can tell what position a journalist may take on any issue. The days of no position passed long, long ago.

They decided to talk to him because Mark insisted that it is important to do so. The meeting was arranged by a phone call from Jimmy's friend the priest at Georgetown University. Jimmy handed a note to the priest, which asked him to give Michael Letsnew a call and explain the purpose for the meeting. The priest did this and Michael recommended that they meet near a restaurant complex at an inlet from Lake Ontario. There was plenty of walking room in that area and it would be easy to talk without being heard. With a smile David had said to Jimmy, "He would know about that since he's a journalist." They both laughed, but they both still had concerns.

They decided to head up to Rochester, New York on Saturday morning. The plan would be to leave early and they would be meeting Michael at the inlet around one o'clock in the afternoon. They left in David's car and headed on Interstate 495 to 95 N. Where they were heading was to Interstate 83 and they would take that route north 81 N. They would be heading towards Williamsport, Pennsylvania. From Williamsport they headed up Route 15 into New York State and then got on the interstates again all the way to Rochester. Neither Jimmy nor Dave had any idea of the beautiful sights through the northern forests of Pennsylvania.

As you drive the road weaves its way through the mountains. The mountains in mid-Pennsylvania look more like waves. They are systematically located one after the other. However, when you reach the tertiary mountains in northern Pennsylvania and lower New York the structure changes. It is an even more beautiful drive. Jimmy laughed when they reached Williamsport. He was thinking about what Mark told him in the restaurant as he explained the proper way of looking at UFOs. He explained it again to David.

David laughed and said, "He was quite accurate."

They drove directly into downtown Rochester and checked in to their room at the Sheraton Hotel. They quickly went back out to their car and headed toward the inlet. When they reached the inlet there was an extremely large parking area with various restaurants and community buildings spread all along the western edge of the inlet.

They were supposed to meet Michael on the walkway that runs along the inlet at a point directly across from a famous lighthouse. As they approached that area, they saw a man alone and leaning on the railing of the walkway. He seemed to be staring out across the inlet. He had salt-and-pepper hair and stood about six feet tall.

As they got close Jimmy said, "Michael?"

The man turned around and looked at them for perhaps one second longer than a person normally would and said, "James? David?"

They shook hands and Jimmy said, "You have a great city."

Michael paused for that long second again and said, "So you don't like our city?"

Jimmy answered, "No I do. Why do you say that?"

Michael pauses again and slowly states, "It's how people say it. People who love it say 'This is a great city. I would love to live here.' You know, things like that. What you said was 'You have a great city.' In other words, I have a great city, but you're not interested. There's nothing wrong with saying it that way. It's cordial. It's a lot better than saying 'you have a terrible city here.'"

"Ah, now I see why Mark focused on you. You are a pure old-time journalist," Jimmy said.

There was a slight smile on Michael's face.

Life is not easy on journalists. They decide their profession for a reason. Their mothers do not like what they do. Neither do their fathers like what they do. Their newspaper employers usually do not like what they do. Their children do not like what they do. Even their pets do not like what they do. They share something with people like Amelia Earhart, John Glenn, Ted Bundy. They fixate. They are trying to uncover the truth and their minds fixate on the search. That is their job. Most people would rather forget certain truths but not the journalists. For them there is no problem with fixation. The only thing they fight is not the truth but rather people who only want their version of the truth.

David asked, "How did he meet you?"

Michael responded, "He didn't meet me. I met him. It's a little complicated. You know that his laboratory, if that's what you want to call it, is in the mountains southwest of here. What's left of it. that is. I heard a rumor that it's gone. I happened to be at an Ace Hardware store in town one day and I heard a man asking the store manager that he is interested in the weakest sensors possible. He wanted 500 of them.

"Now that piqued my interest," Michael said. "You see, I realize that both of you are scientists. I'm not a scientist. I suspect that neither of you would have been interested in hearing a man ask for something of low sensitivity. He was asking for it not because he wanted low quality. Now, since I'm not a scientist and I'm a journalist, that captured my attention. To a lesser extent the actual items that he was searching for immediately drew my attention as well. I waited until the customer obtained what he was looking for and he turned toward the door. I introduced myself to him and tried to see if he was willing to tell me why he wanted that item. The man was Robert. Do you know who he is?"

David said, "No."

Jimmy said, "Oh, I think I know who he is. I met him through Mark a long time ago and if he is the Robert that I'm thinking about, I'm willing to bet that you didn't learn anything except his name. Am I correct?"

Michael responded, "Oh, you're quite right. However, you now had a journalist who is even more interested in something and had to solve it. We have a way in journalism of getting information on people, places, and things. I wrote down his license plate number. I spoke to the man at the Ace Hardware and I was on my way to eventually meeting Mark. A few weeks later I was knocking on the door to the laboratory or whatever it was. If you are going to ask me, the journalist, if I knew exactly what was going on in this situation the answer is no I did not. Or at least I did not know until one day a year later when without me specifically asking, Mark explained the entire project to me. He trusted me. That trust is extremely valuable to a journalist. As time went by, I began to wish that I had known Mark years before. It was just like, Jimmy, so many people wished to know your grandmother Tillie. Yes, you can imagine where our talks visited. I feel the same way about your grandmother and I never met her. She had more influence on Mark's whole thought process than any individual."

He continued. "I remember that first day when I found my way to the laboratory. I drove on a gravel road for fifteen miles. Then I reached a small lake. That is where I left the car. There was a sign that said *A. R. G.* and an arrow pointing into what I thought were simply the woods but there was a path. I followed the path more deeply into the woods. Then I heard a waterfall. The fir tree scent was intense. I continued to a small island next to the falls. There stood a sixty- foot-high granite rock protruding from the side of the mountain. The waterfall originated higher up in the mountain. There, in front of me was a door going into the rock. Get this… there was a doorbell. I rang it and Mark came to the door. He had a smile on his face and said to me 'Ah. Robert told me you would come visiting us some day.'

"Initially, he told me that they actually were working on a detection system that would spread out in distance as far as you would want to be detecting any motion of any living thing. Eventually Mark explained how it would work. It did work. It was truly amazing. Initially, though, that laboratory seemed to be about 100 yards in length. However, as to the real work going on, it was quite hidden. The laboratory looked like it was built into the side of the mountain and it was actually a large portion of the mountain that was being reconstructed.

"When I entered, I never knew the actual size until he finally told me. I then got to see it. To this day I, as a journalist, am not certain if I could ever fully describe it. Every aspect of it contained machines I had never seen. There were things that I truly did not recognize. Some were explained to me. I asked him where he learned to construct one machine the purpose of which was to control distraction of electronic force. He changed the subject and did not answer."

Michael was quiet for a second or two and then said, "He had been given help. No question about that. I am not saying that I know anything about your expertise except as he explained certain things about the vessel it seemed as if unbelievable surges of his ability to know what he was building took place almost over a weekend."

Jimmy asked, "Did you ask him if he had contact with anyone or anything?"

Michael responded, "Of course I did. I am a reporter."

Jimmy continued his question, "What did he say when you asked him that question?"

Michael said, "He simply kept saying 'we came to understand' and that was his answer over and over again."

Jimmy and David looked at each other and nodded and looked at Michael and said, "We agree with you." Then Jimmy asked, "Why did he befriend you?"

Michael answered, "He wanted me to be the one who organized release of information to all press... all over the world. I started the moment I heard that something may have happened at the lab."

CHAPTER 26

Mark had a plan that had been discussed between a select few people. It had actually started into action months before Mark returned to life in the visit to Jimmy in the restaurant in New York City. He never told anyone the entire story. That was promised to Jimmy. Attorney John Murtaugh was contracted by Mark and his group early as soon as they realized the objections they would receive from the people who governmentally run the large countries. They understood what they would likely need to do to protect the people on this planet who must have this information.

Murtaugh purposefully stayed out of the picture after that meeting. Everyone knew that his skills were going to be needed and he must not be connected to the rest until the time was right. After the meeting with Lynn and Melinda, transfer of information to each individual was carried out through Dr. Brennan and his wife, Fawn.

The Lateral Thinking and preparation of any person interested in concepts of an unusual type of thought was carried out by Edward Malm. What Ed Malm actually did was astounding. He actually was able to change human beings' feelings about space beings and space travel from fear to acceptance. He had friends write books that pushed the reader in that direction. He had people in the movie industry produce movies where the extraterrestrial being was more like the one in the movie *E.T.* Michael was asked to prepare the news industry by working with Ed. Finally, Jimmy, Melinda, David, and Lynn were notified through Brennan and Fawn that everything regarding the release of all of the information on the chip was in motion.

Newspapers, radio stations, television networks, and the internet were all contacted at the exact same time. In addition, all religions were contacted at multiple levels. Individual countries were contacted. Each entity received the same information that Mark had passed on to the group. There was too much information spread to thousands of sites around the planet so that no single country or government could claim possession of the information that Mark and his group had uncovered. Perhaps most important of all was the building plans of the vessel itself. It could be constructed much less expensively than anyone could ever imagine.

The cost is in building the first vessel. That is what Mark's crew had accomplished. Vessels built afterward would be much less costly. The explanation of travel inside the 'In Between" is not like travel in our universe. There is no time. There is no weightlessness.

The plan was to start sending the information through every means possible. That included internet, hand-to-hand passage, national, and international mail. Every possible pathway was used so that there would be no way to stop the spreading of the information to everyone on the planet.

The results were exactly as Murtaugh predicted. The people, the press, the religions were initially questioning the information but as their experts looked into the information on the chip the attitude began to change. The governments of all powerful countries were angry. The other countries were pleased.

In the larger completely government-controlled countries there would be arrests. This accomplished nothing. The information continued to spread. In most countries the story was incessantly discussed on the news and anywhere that people congealed. In the non-freedom countries it was incessantly spread mouth-to-mouth. In the end no one was left out.

The entire group from the United States including all connected to the information on the chip were brought in for interrogation. Once that began the group hired Attorney John Murtaugh to defend them.

The people of the planet Earth knew exactly why the information was spread to everyone. That way the information could not be used as a weapon. It would be governments who were interested in using the information in that manner. Not the people, though they saw each other.

Attempts to contact UFOs increased, but to no avail. The UFOs were here and then they would leave. Later, new ones would arrive and they also had no interest in contact.

The religions had been slightly concerned at the beginning, but they then realized that this information is directly involved with everything they had been teaching. There was no threat to the religion. There was only strengthening. Certain parts of the mystery of faith may now be understood. The strength of that faith increased. It increased in all religions far beyond anybody's imagination.

Chapter 27

It was a beautiful day in October when the hearings began at the New York State Supreme Court. The United States government was attempting to charge the group which included Jimmy, Melinda, David, Lynn, Ed, Michael, Father Consolo, Brennan, and Fawn with a supposed crime against the United States of America. The crime that they were attempting to create was espionage and sharing top-secret information. Attorney Murtaugh had prepared for this three years before. He knew that there could not be such a crime since the United States Government never possessed the information. However, he also knew that constitutional law never stops governments from breaking the Constitution.

The trial proceeded every day from 9:00 A.M. to 4:00 P.M. The government only allowed certain segments to be videotaped. The prosecution had already brought forth FBI agents, CIA agents, military leaders, other scientists, psychologists and anyone else that they could convince to testify against the group.

Murtaugh told each individual that they should not testify because there is no crime. Virtually all attorneys in the United States of America agreed with Murtaugh's stance. This did not stop the government.

Some of the testimony put forth by the prosecution witnesses had no basis in truth. The group's position as United States citizens was

135

questioned but in every case Murtaugh unraveled the United States Government's position and put forth the real truth that these people were United States citizens who were concerned about all humans.

On this day the judge had a concerned expression on his face. The group members each had a concerned expression on their faces and the prosecution seemed to feel happy that they were making some progress against the group.

A witness from the United States Postal Service was being questioned about the legality of the spread of the information, when, suddenly, the door at the back of the courtroom opened and in walked a woman. She came to the top of the center aisle and stopped. Everyone in the courtroom turned toward her. No one knew who she was. No one knew why she was standing in the center aisle. Then suddenly an enormous smile breaks across her face and in a loud voice she says "They are back!"

Everybody in the group being investigated turned toward each other and slowly smiles began to spread across their faces and they grabbed on to each other whispering, "They are back!"

The judges turned to look at each other and smiles broke out on their faces.

The prosecution table looked bewildered.

The head judge reached forward and grabbed the gavel and raised it over his head. He brought it down.

They are back.